BADLANDS GOLD RUSH

Also by Eldridge James and published by Catnip:

Death in Drygulch

Range Wars

ELDRIDGE JAMES

Catnip

To those cowboys in the
making, Jack and Albert,
with love from their
Grandpa Jim

CATNIP BOOKS
Published by Catnip Publishing Ltd
14 Greville Street
London
EC1N 8SB

This edition first published 2011

1 3 5 7 9 10 8 6 4 2

Cover photo of Billy Joe by butterworthdesign.com
Additional background photo from iStockphoto

A CIP catalogue record for this book is available from the British Library.

ISBN 978-1-84647-113-1

Printed in Poland

www.catnippublishing.co.uk

CHAPTER 1

*B*ang! Billy Joe Ford froze in his tracks as the gunshot echoed through the night. It could have been one of the prospectors shooting at a coyote, but Billy Joe knew in his bones it wasn't. Hunters usually fired more than once. A single shot meant a gunman.

'Andy!' he whispered urgently, as loud as he dare.

There was no answer.

Tiny Andy, six years old, had vanished from their tent. That was typical of Andy. He was always going off wandering on his own, no matter how many times they told him not to. Now there was a gunman out there, and in the pitch-black darkness of the thicket Andy was likely to stumble into him and get himself shot.

'Andy!' he called again, still in a whisper, but just a bit louder.

'Billy Joe? That you?' came Andy's small voice.

'Who else do you think would be fool enough to come out here lookin' for you at this time of night?' demanded Billy Joe angrily.

Andy appeared out of the gloom.

'I was lookin' for Patch,' he said. Patch was the gang's dog, a half-deaf stray who was as likely to wander off and get into trouble as Andy, although not tonight.

'Patch is back at the tent,' said Billy Joe. 'He come back soon after you disappeared.'

'I didn't disappear!' protested Andy. Then his tone grew concerned. 'Did you hear that shot?'

'I sure did,' said Billy Joe. 'So it makes sense for us to head back before whoever fired it starts shootin' again. In this dark they might just shoot us by mistake.'

Billy Joe reached out to take Andy's hand, but Andy shook him off.

'I ain't no baby, Billy Joe,' he said crossly. 'I don't need no one to hold my hand!'

'No, you need tyin' up,' snapped Billy Joe. 'Now stick close to me and don't go runnin' off again!'

The two boys headed slowly through the trees towards where their tent was pitched, at the edge of the small township of temporary dwellings that had sprung up around the goldfields.

Wherever we are, we're always on the outside, thought Billy Joe. In the town of Drygulch, where the small gang of four boys lived, their house was on the edge of town. Here at the goldfields, it was no different.

As the trees thinned out, Andy stumbled and then fell with a yell.

'Tarnation, Andy!' cursed Billy Joe. 'Can't you even walk straight?'

'I fell over somethin',' said Andy defensively, pushing himself to his feet. Then his tone changed and Billy Joe heard the shake in his voice. 'I think it's a body.'

'Move away from it,' Billy Joe ordered. 'But stay where I can see you!'

As Andy moved slowly backwards, Billy Joe hurried to where the small boy had been standing. Sure enough, there was a body there, lying face down. A man. One of the prospectors by the look of his clothes, which were all dirty and stained from panning for gold in the river. With a trembling hand Billy Joe reached out and touched the man's neck, feeling for a pulse. There was none.

Billy Joe's eyes were getting used to the dark now. The moonlight filtering through the canopy of the trees helped. Now it was reflecting on something wet on the man's back. Billy Joe reached out and touched it, but he knew what it was already. Blood.

'Is he dead?' asked Andy nervously.

'Yep,' nodded Billy Joe. He stood up. 'We'd better get back to the tent and tell Jess and Shane.'

'Ain't you gonna turn him over and see who he is?' asked Andy.

'Nope,' said Billy Joe. 'Let someone else do that.

The main thing is, it ain't one of us.'

He headed for the small township of tents, Andy staying close behind him. With a dead man on the ground, there was no chance of Andy straying off this time.

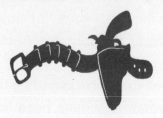

CHAPTER 2

The other two boys in the gang were sitting outside the tent brewing coffee on a wood fire as Billy Joe and Andy hurried over. Patch was lying down beside them, but at the sight of Andy he leapt up and bounded towards his friend, his tongue lolling in delight. The gang's leader, fourteen-year-old Jess may have been the one who had found Patch, but they all knew he considered himself to be Andy's dog.

'You found him then!' said Jess. Turning to Andy, he said sharply, 'I told you not to go runnin' off like that! There's dangerous people round here!'

'There sure are,' said Billy Joe grimly. 'We just found a man shot dead.'

'Wh-what?' exclaimed Shane, shocked. 'Wh-where?'

'Just up by the thicket,' said Billy Joe, pointing towards the small wood.

'Who is he?' asked Jess.

'I don't know,' said Billy Joe. 'He was shot in the back and I didn't turn him over to look. I thought it best to come and tell you. If people find me covered in blood, they could go sayin' I killed him. You know what they're like.'

Jess nodded. Since Billy Joe had joined their small gang just six months before, he'd shot two men. On both occasions he'd had no choice – it had been pull the trigger or risk his own life or that of his friends. But as a consequence he'd gained a reputation as a killer. On the one hand it meant that people stayed away from him, not wanting to tangle with an eleven-year-old boy who'd shot and killed two notorious gunmen. But it also meant that people considered Billy Joe to be Big Trouble, and they wanted nothing to do with him.

'You all stay here,' said Jess. 'I'll go and get Mr Vernon.'

John Vernon was the person most people went to when things went wrong at the goldfields, or to sort out arguments between prospectors. A tall quiet man with a big moustache, he commanded respect just by his manner. He was the sort of man people felt they could talk to and he'd listen, and do his best to *do* something.

As Jess hurried off to the tent where Vernon and his wife lived, near the centre of the settlement, Billy Joe joined Shane beside the fire. Andy and Patch dumped themselves down on the ground close by.

'Y-you reckon it w-was a g-gunfight?' whispered Shane. He was a couple of years younger than Billy Joe, but like all the boys he was no stranger to the real world.

Billy Joe shook his head.

'I only heard one shot. And this man was shot in the back. It was murder.'

'Wh-who'd do s-somethin' like that?'

But they both had a good idea of the person who might shoot a man in the back. Especially if that man was carrying gold. Duke Rixon was a gunfighter employed by a businessman called Sam Farley. Farley didn't do any searching for gold himself, although he had a claim that two men worked for him. Farley's main business was setting up what he called a 'Prospectors' Cooperative'.

His idea was that the prospectors should band together for help and protection. That the more of them there who were working together, the safer they'd be against claim jumpers and robbers. To join the Cooperative, prospectors paid twenty dollars, plus they had to agree to pay a quarter of any gold they found. According to Farley, this would cover running costs of the Cooperative and pay for their protection. The protection took the form of a group of gunmen led by Duke Rixon, who'd arrived with Farley when he came to stake his claim at the goldfields.

Most of the prospectors had turned down Farley's

offer. The truth was that few of them could afford to pay twenty dollars, and if they found gold by their own hard work and sweat, they didn't want to have to give a quarter of it away. It hadn't gone unnoticed that Farley's claim was a small one and not likely to produce much. Many people suspected that Farley was just there to make money from the prospectors, not by panning for gold.

It was John Vernon who'd been the most vocal in saying this out loud, both to the other prospectors and to Farley himself. Yesterday the boys had seen yet another confrontation between Farley and Vernon, and noticed the way that Duke Rixon had glared at the outspoken prospector, his fingers hovering just above his holster, ready to draw.

Vernon himself had laughed out loud.

'You gonna shoot me, Rixon?' he demanded. 'You gonna shoot an unarmed man in front of all these witnesses?'

Farley had chuckled at this, though his laughter had sounded false to Billy Joe.

'Why would Duke wanna shoot you, Mr Vernon?' he said. 'He only shoots bad guys to protect decent law-abiding folk.'

Billy Joe looked at Rixon, and thought, *That's a stone-cold lie. Rixon is one real bad guy. I can see it in his face. He's a hothead who likes killing, and he don't care who he shoots.*

Billy Joe looked up to see people gathering around the spot where he and Andy had found the dead man. Jess had obviously found John Vernon and some of the other prospectors and persuaded them to join him in going to where the body lay. There didn't seem to be many of them though, only about five.

Suddenly a woman's wail came from the group of people, a howl of grief and misery that was so painful it sent a shiver down Billy Joe's back.

'Wh-what was th-that?' asked Shane, shaken.

Patch began to bark and Andy put both his arms round the dog and cuddled him close, calming him down. They were aware of Jess running towards them, limping slightly as he ran, a permanent reminder of the time he'd been badly shot in the leg by gunmen. He reached their tent, out of breath.

'It's John Vernon!' he announced. 'The dead man is Mr Vernon!'

CHAPTER 3

As the sun rose the next morning, Jess, Billy Joe, Shane and Andy, with Patch in tow, joined some of the other prospectors at the tent where Abbey Vernon was loading her belongings onto a buckboard. The body of her husband was already lying on the back of the buckboard, covered in a linen sheet. Some of the prospectors were helping her take down her tent, while others helped her carry her possessions to the buggy. All of them found it impossible not to look at the shape of the body lying beneath the linen sheet that had been tied up to stop it flapping and blowing away.

Jess approached Abbey Vernon, the rest of the gang behind him.

'I'd just like to say we're sorry for your loss, Mrs Vernon,' he said. 'Mr Vernon was a real good friend to us.'

Abbey Vernon looked at the boys and nodded in acknowledgement.

'John's problem was that he tried to be a real good friend to everyone, taking up everyone's business, and in the end it got him killed.' She shook her head sadly. 'But I wouldn't have wanted him to be any other way. He was strong and honest and he didn't scare off. And there ain't many folks you can say that about.' She looked at Jess thoughtfully. 'You're like my John was though, Jess. You got that same way about you. I admire that. Some day you're gonna make some woman a very good husband. I hope she appreciates you as much as I appreciated my John.'

Jess dropped his head and Billy Joe could see his friend's ears had turned red. *Jess is blushing*! he thought. But Billy Joe agreed with Mrs Vernon – just like Mr Vernon had been, Jess was a natural leader, and Billy Joe was proud to have him for his friend.

'Y-you d-don't have to g-go, M-Mrs Vernon,' said Shane. 'We c-can l-look after you.'

Abbey Vernon smiled a small, sad smile.

'That's very kind of you, Shane, but without John this ain't no place for me. I was quite happy workin' our farm. We never made much money, but it was quiet and that's the way I liked it. John thought we could make our fortune here.' She looked around at the small township of tents and shook her head. 'There ain't no fortunes bein' made here. There's only death.'

'That ain't true, Abbey,' said one of the prospectors, Jasper Wade. 'Robert here panned some gold from the creek only the other day. Ain't that right, Robert?'

A young man with a stubbly beard, Robert Jackson, nodded.

'There ain't enough gold in the world to pay fer my husband being killed,' said Abbey.

The sound of horses' hooves made them all turn. Sam Farley was on his horse. Behind him rode Duke Rixon and his gunmen, five grim men with sour faces, grubby shirts and fast guns. They pulled their horses to a halt and Farley dismounted. Most of the prospectors backed away as he approached Abbey Vernon and the buggy.

Farley took off his hat.

'I've come here to pay my respects, Mrs Vernon,' he said. 'I heard about the tragedy.'

Billy Joe did his best to stop the sneer of disbelief showing on his face. He turned to Jess, whose expression remained impassive, but he could see from the look in his friend's eyes that he felt the same way as Billy Joe. Everyone knew that one of Farley's men had gunned down John Vernon. Worse, they'd shot him in the back.

Abbey Vernon didn't answer. She just glared directly back at Farley, and he could see the fury in her eyes. He turned away awkwardly and addressed the other prospectors.

'Like I say, this is a tragedy!' Farley proclaimed, his voice loud. 'This is the sort of thing that happens when there's gold around and a fortune to be made. That's why we all need the protection I'm offering. Whoever killed John Vernon is still out there!'

'He sure is,' snapped Abbey Vernon. 'And I'm lookin' right at him!'

A gasp went through the prospectors as they turned towards her. She was glaring directly at Duke Rixon.

Rixon scowled.

'Are you accusin' me?' he demanded angrily.

'You're the hired gun,' said Abbey Vernon. 'You and the scum with you!'

'Why you –' snarled Rixon. He started to pull his gun out of its holster, but was stopped by a shout from Farley.

'That's enough!' barked Farley. He turned to Abbey Vernon, his tone softer and his face showing an expression of concern. 'Ma'am, I understand you're sufferin' grief right now, but that's no call to go makin' unfair and unjust accusations.'

Abbey spat on the ground in disgust.

'Unfair and unjust?' she repeated sarcastically. 'That gunman of yours killed my John because he stood up to you, and everyone here knows it. If any man here had an ounce of guts he'd be shootin' your man down right now fer the lyin' cowardly dog he is.' She shook her head. 'But there's no law and no justice here. Now, if your weasel of a gunman there wants to shoot me down in cold blood like he did my husband, so be it. I'll even turn around so he can shoot me in the back the same way.'

Billy Joe glanced at Rixon. He could see the gunman's hand clenching and unclenching near his gun.

Farley shook his head.

'Mrs Vernon, like I said, you're a woman eaten up by grief, so we'll make allowances right now for your unjust name callin' –'

Abbey Vernon didn't let him finish.

'If I had me a gun there'd be more than words I'd be throwin' at you and your hired scum,' she said. She stopped, and then did her best to calm down rather than lose her temper. 'But right now I ain't got no more time to waste. I have to get back to my home and bury this good man.'

With that, she flicked the reins, and her horse began to move forward.

CHAPTER 4

As the crowds parted to let the buckboard pass, Billy Joe saw the exchange of looks that passed between Farley and Rixon, the older man warning Rixon to behave. As the buggy disappeared from the edge of the township of tents, Farley addressed the gathered prospectors again.

'Like I was saying, the shooting of John Vernon was a tragedy, but it's one that could have been avoided. That's what the Prospectors' Cooperative is here for. If John Vernon had joined up for protection, he'd still be alive this morning, instead of being taken home for burial.'

Billy Joe looked around at the prospectors. All of them seemed uncomfortable. Most of them looked like they wanted to get away, but they were scared of upsetting Farley. Or, more exactly, they were scared of upsetting Duke Rixon.

'So I urge you, join up with the Cooperative and make sure you and your family are safe!' Farley continued.

'And give you a quarter share of whatever we find,' murmured Jess quietly.

There was no doubt that Jess's jibe, although spoken quietly, had stung Farley. He scowled momentarily, then the scowl vanished and was replaced by his automatic smile.

'A quarter share, son, plus fifty dollars joining fee,' he said.

'*Fifty* dollars!' protested Jasper Wade. 'It was twenty dollars yesterday!'

'That was before John Vernon was shot and killed,' said Farley. 'Things are more dangerous now. We know for sure there's a killer loose in the area. Probably more than one.'

Probably at least six of them, thought Billy Joe, counting Duke Rixon and his five gunmen.

'If you take my advice, you'll sign up for the Cooperative today, while the joining fee is still just fifty dollars.'

'But none of us here have fifty dollars!' Wade shouted out. 'If we did, we wouldn't likely be here!'

Farley shrugged.

'I'm happy to take any man's marker and count it as a loan, just like I do at the store.' He walked back to his horse and jumped in the saddle. 'Remember, today the joining fee is fifty dollars. If there's any more killings, the price is likely to go up. Good protection don't come cheap.'

With that, Farley trotted away.

Rixon looked at the prospectors and gave them an ugly smile.

'I'd take note of that good advice from Mr Farley,' he said. 'Before anyone else gets shot.'

He grinned and pointedly patted the gun at his side, then gave a shout and pulled his horse round. He and the five other gunmen rode off at speed after Farley, the hooves of their horses sending up a cloud of dust as they went.

As soon as they'd gone, a babble of loud and angry chatter burst out.

'What we gonna do?' demanded one.

'Pay up,' said another miserably. 'What choice do we have?'

'We could get a lawman in, tell him what's going on?' suggested yet another.

'There ain't no law here!' snapped Wade. 'This here's Marshall territory, and by the time the Marshall arrives Rixon and Farley will have killed off any witnesses, or anyone who's got a complaint to make.'

'So what are you suggesting? That we just pay up to that crook?' the young prospector, Robert Jackson, asked angrily.

'Well, you could always do what John Vernon did

and stand up to him,' said Wade. 'So long as you don't mind getting shot in the back.'

'But this is wrong!' said Jackson. 'There's plenty of us and just six of them! I say we get us some guns and defend ourselves.'

'Rixon and his gang are hired gunmen,' said Wade. 'You wouldn't stand a chance against them if it came to a gunfight.'

'Then why don't we get us a gunfighter of our own?' asked Jimmy Flynn, an older prospector, all grizzled beard and matted hair.

Wade laughed.

'We ain't got the money to pay Farley,' he snorted. 'How are we gonna pay a gunfighter?'

'We get one that's cheap,' said Flynn.

'Cheap means no good,' countered Wade. 'And one gunfighter ain't gonna be much use against six.'

'The gunfighter I'm thinking of would be,' said Flynn. 'Fastest draw I ever seen. Name of Kelly. Quick and as accurate a shot as anyone you're likely to see.'

Billy Joe could see that Flynn's suggestion, and his description of the gunfighter Kelly, had roused interest in some of the prospectors. Others, though, shook their heads.

'It won't work,' said one gloomily. 'I hear many tales about how this gunfighter or that gunfighter is the fastest ever, but most of the time it's just tales and boasting.'

'We get ourselves a gunfighter, we might find ourselves in worse trouble,' said Wade. 'As soon as Farley and Rixon find out about it they'll come here, shoot this Kelly, and then charge us a hundred dollars each and a half share in our gold stakes. Better to pay up now while the price ain't so high.'

'It seems to me you give up awful easy, Mr Wade,' said Jess, speaking up for the first time.

The crowd fell silent as Wade turned to Jess and studied him.

'Son, I'm gonna ignore that remark on account of you bein' just a boy and knowin' nothin' about life,' he said. 'Trust me, I've been all over this land, and one thing I've learnt – the big and powerful rule it and they take what they want, and no one can touch 'em. If you try and stand in their way, like poor John Vernon did, you just get shot down.'

'With respect, Mr Wade,' said Jess levelly, 'it seems we ought to at least take a look at this gunfighter Mr Flynn is talking about. If he's as good as Mr Flynn says it'd be cheaper for us to pay him to protect us, rather than pay Farley's price – fifty dollars each to Farley is a whole lot of money in one man's pocket. I don't mind payin' a fair price to a good worker, but I'm damned if I'm gonna give a quarter of what I earn by my sweat and muscle to someone just cos he bullies me into it. And I think I can say the same for the rest of my boys.'

'You sure can, Jess!' piped up little Andy.

At hearing Andy call out, Wade laughed out loud.

'That's about the size of it, son,' he said. 'The only people who think like that are little kids who don't know no better and never seen the business end of a gun.'

'That ain't so!' retorted Andy. 'Billy Joe here shot two bad gunmen when they was threatenin' us!'

An awkward silence fell over the crowd and all eyes turned to Billy Joe, many of them looking at him with suspicion.

Damn Andy and his big mouth! cursed Billy Joe silently.

'That so, son?' asked Wade. 'You mean we got a killer among us?'

'Maybe the boy will be our gunfighter?' called out one of the prospectors, and then laughed to show he was only joking.

Billy Joe noticed that not everyone joined in his laughter, some of them were still looking at him with suspicion and concern in their eyes.

'Enough of this – I object to my opinion being lumped with a bunch of kids!' barked Flynn. Then he realised what he'd said, because he turned to Andy and the boys and added apologetically, 'Not that I meant anythin' by that – you're the only ones talkin' sense right now.'

'No offence taken, Mr Flynn,' said Jess quickly, and grabbed Andy to shut him up because he could tell his friend was about to protest about being called a little kid.

'Like I was sayin', I bin around a long time,' continued Flynn, 'and I knows a good gunfighter when I see one, and this here Kelly is one of the best. I saw her in action in Tuscon. Fastest draw I ever seen.'

There was a stunned silence among the crowd, a silence finally broken by Jackson repeating, '*Her*?'

'No woman can protect us against Rixon and his gang,' protested one of the men.

'She can,' insisted Flynn. 'Like I say, I seen her in action, and I asked about her around. She's honest and she won't take our money and run off, like some o' them so-called gunfighters.'

Wade shook his head.

'You wanna hire her, Jimmy Flynn, you're on your own. Me, I'd rather give my money to Farley while the price is still reasonable. That way I can stay alive.'

'We'll come in with you, Mr Flynn,' said Jess. Turning to Billy Joe and Shane he asked, 'Won't we?'

Shane nodded.

'W-we s-sure w-will!' he said determinedly.

Billy Joe stayed silent. He thought it was a fool idea. The more he thought about it, even just being here at the goldfields was a fool idea. They'd be better off back in Drygulch, cleaning stables and stuff and getting paid real money.

'You can count me in too, Mr Flynn,' said young Robert Jackson. 'If Kelly's as good as you say she is, it'll be worth it.'

Other prospectors could be heard murmuring their assent too. Jasper Wade shook his head in disgust and spat on the ground.

'You're a bunch of fools, every one of you!' he snapped. 'I'm gonna sign up with Farley. Who's with me?'

There was a moment's hesitation, then some of the prospectors awkwardly moved away and went to join Wade. Slowly, more followed them, until finally there were just Jimmy Flynn, Robert Jackson, Jess and the gang, and four others standing together.

Flynn gave them all a big smile.

'Well, there ain't as many of us as I'd hoped, but once Kitty Kelly gets here and shows what she can do, I'm sure some of them folks will come back and join us again!'

'You're living in dreamland, Jimmy Flynn,' snorted Wade.

With that, he set off, followed by most of the other prospectors, and headed towards Sam Farley's camp.

Billy Joe shook his head. 'Looks like we've landed ourselves right in the middle of a gun war,' he muttered.

CHAPTER 5

The next two days saw the gang working their claim on the goldfields. The site where everyone was looking for gold ran along the course of a shallow, slow-moving stream that twisted and turned as it ran through a deep gulley.

All along the whole four-mile length, claims had been staked out. Jess, Billy Joe and Shane had marked the edge of their patch by driving bits of broken branches from trees into the mud at the side of the stream, and then up to the top of the gulley. They'd sharpened the ends of the rough branches like fencing posts, then hammered them into the ground. That done, they'd tied rope between the rough posts, just to make sure that no one 'accidentally' started searching for gold across the dividing line on their claim.

Panning for signs of gold was a long and boring job. The boys took it in turn to stand at the edge of the stream and catch the slow-moving muddy water in flat-bottomed pans. They would carefully drain out the water, leaving silt behind in the pan. Then they picked over the silt with their fingers, looking for anything that glistened in the mud.

Some people claimed to have found small nuggets this way. Others had found tiny specks of gold, which when dried turned into gold dust. And lots of dried gold dust meant good money. Whether it was in nugget form or dust form it was all still gold.

As well as panning, they also dug for gold in the walls of the gulley on their side of the stream. The boys' claim ended halfway across the stream. The young prospector, Robert Jackson, had the claim that went from the middle of the stream up the other bank. Billy Joe was glad they had Robert as their neighbour and not some of the other prospectors, who were mean and selfish.

Mostly it was Andy and Shane who panned the stream, while Jess and Billy Joe dug at the soil; but every now and then they changed over, so Billy Joe and Jess spent time kneeling by the edge of the water, while Shane and Andy dug and scratched at the rocky sandy soil, with Patch jumping around and getting in the way.

* * *

Things seemed to go quiet after the death of John Vernon. Jasper Wade and most of the other prospectors made no secret of the fact that they'd gone along to see Sam Farley and had signed up for his Cooperative. It was also no secret that Jess and the gang, Robert, Jimmy Flynn and four others had not signed up, but were continuing to prospect for gold.

Although everything seemed to be quiet, Billy Joe was pretty sure it wouldn't be long before things turned nasty. He knew that the longer people like them carried on prospecting without paying anything to Sam Farley and his men, it would send out a message that it was a waste of money. Because of this, Billy Joe had said he wanted to keep a gun to defend themselves.

Jess had argued against it strongly.

'Look at it this way, Billy Joe. After what Andy said, there's already people here think of you as a killer.'

'That ain't my fault,' said Billy Joe. 'You and I know it was self-defence both times and that's all I'm talking about now – defending ourselves.'

'You know that near every time someone shoots someone they claim it was self-defence. Ain't no one believes that no more.'

'Them not believin' it don't make it any less true!' Billy Joe sighed, then decided to try another tack. 'Duke Rixon and his men carry guns like they was goin' to war, and they plan to use 'em. Probably on us.'

'I know, Billy Joe,' said Jess, 'which is even more

reason why you shouldn't be packin' a gun. Once it gets out that you've got a gun, those gunmen'll use it as an excuse to shoot you. And they'll claim self-defence, you can be sure of that.'

The argument had left Billy Joe feeling frustrated. Part of him knew that everything Jess said was right. But another part knew that one day Duke Rixon would come gunning for the gang, and when that time came Billy Joe wanted to know he had a good way of defending himself. Throwing rocks at Rixon wouldn't do it. A gun would. As he pointed out to Jess, 'If you're so against guns, why you agreein' to hire this Kitty Kelly gunfighter?'

'Because that's what she does, according to Jimmy Flynn. That's her job. Just like it's the Sheriff's job to take care of bad guys. That's what he practises with a gun for. It's not our job. We try it, we'll get ourselves killed for sure. Trust me, Billy Joe. I'm doin' this for you.'

And Billy Joe knew that Jess was right. And so he'd taken a momentous decision. He'd gone to his bedroll and taken out the precious pistol he'd hidden when they'd first come to the goldfields, and handed it over to Jess.

'Here, Jess,' he told him. 'Better stash this somewhere safe where I can't get my hands on it.'

Jess hesitated, holding the pistol in his hand. He wasn't surprised at Billy Joe producing the gun;

he'd guessed that his friend had hidden one away somewhere, but he was surprised at Billy Joe handing it over like this. He knew just how big this decision was for him.

'I'll look after it for you, Billy Joe,' he promised.

And then the two boys shook hands on it.

I just hope I've made the right choice, thought Billy Joe.

CHAPTER 6

It was on the third day after John Vernon had been shot that Jess announced they had problems.

'See that breakfast you got,' he said, indicating the flat cornbread each boy had on his wooden platter. 'Well, that's the last of it.'

'You mean we ain't got no more food?' asked Andy, horrified. 'What we gonna eat?'

'W-we'll d-do what we always d-do,' said Shane. 'We'll g-go c-catch us a rabbit or s-somethin'.'

Jess shook his head. They all knew that catching rabbits had become harder now that the rabbits were wise to the settlers hunting them.

'I can try, as well as pick us some berries an' stuff, an' we still got some beef jerky we brung with us from Drygulch, but we need flour,' he said.

The boys fell silent. They knew what this meant. The only provisions available near the tented town were from Farley's Supply Store – two wagons of supplies that Sam Farley had set up as a store on wheels at the edge of the goldfields. The wagons weren't like the covered wagons that most people had, they were proper buildings on wheels, pulled by four horses each. Inside, Sam Farley had everything a prospector could want – food, rope, tools, guns and ammunition, but they cost money. And Farley made sure that everything in his store was marked at top price.

The alternative was to go to Drygulch, but Drygulch was two days' ride away; four days travelling and one day in Drygulch to rest the horses. Most prospectors couldn't afford to be away from their claim for as long as five days. In that time there was the chance of someone else moving in on it. So people gritted their teeth and went to Farley's Supply Store and paid his exorbitant prices.

So far the boys had been able to get by without buying new supplies. They'd brought a good store of dried foodstuffs with them to the goldfields – beef jerky, dried meat and fish, dried fruit and nuts, all of which stayed fresh and edible, if a bit chewy. They'd also brought a sack of cornflour, which was their staple. But now – according to Jess – that was just about gone.

'We got to go to Farley's wagons and get us some more flour,' said Jess. 'It's gonna need two of us to carry it back, so I suggest that's you and me, Billy Joe.'

Billy Joe looked down at the cornbread on his platter.

'We got any money to buy it with?' he asked.

Jess shook his head.

'Nope,' he said. 'We're gonna have to ask for credit.'

The boys looked miserable. To ask for credit would mean asking Sam Farley for a favour, something that stuck in the throat of all of them. Worse, they'd pay extra for it, on top of his high prices.

Billy Joe sighed.

'Guess we got no choice,' he said unhappily.

'We always got a choice,' said Jess. 'We either go to Farley's or take a five-day trip to Drygulch.'

Billy Joe nodded, as choices went, this one was a no-brainer.

'OK,' he said. 'Let me finish this, then we'll go see Farley.'

He picked up his cornbread and began to chew slowly on it. Just in case things didn't work out at Farley's wagons, he wanted to savour the flavour so he could remember it.

* ** *

Jess and Billy Joe left Shane looking after Andy and Patch at the claim.

'Don't do no pannin' in the stream while we ain't here,' Jess had warned Shane before they left. 'Else you can be sure that Andy or Patch will fall in and get washed away and drowned.'

'The water ain't deep enough for us to drown!' Andy had protested.

'I heard of a man who drowned in a puddle of water,' retorted Jess. 'So you stay up on the side of the gulley and dig with Patch, and do what Shane tells you.'

As the two boys made their way through the township of tents, Billy Joe cast a glance back.

'Think Andy will do what you told him?' he asked.

'So long as that fool dog stays out of the water, he will,' said Jess.

Billy Joe smiled to himself. Jess spoke disparagingly about 'that fool dog', but he was as fond of the half-deaf Patch as any of the gang. And as long as they were all together that was what really mattered. Even if being together meant working all day out in the heat, getting blisters on their hands and worrying about receiving a bullet in the back.

They soon reached Farley's Supply Store. The wagons looked like a storefront on any street in any Western town, except they had steps that went up from the ground. One of the wagons contained food and groceries, the other had hardware; it even had small barrels of explosives for those who wanted to blast the ground of their claim and speed up the prospecting process.

Sam Farley was standing outside the grocery wagon,

talking to a skinny unkempt girl a bit older than Jess, who acted as his storekeeper. They stopped talking as Jess and Billy Joe arrived.

Farley smiled at the boys. *The same smile that pretended to be friendly, but had no real feeling in it at all*, thought Billy Joe. But Farley's eyes held the truth – they were small, piggy and greedy-looking.

'Well, well, I do believe we have customers.' Farley's voice sounded sly. 'Is that right, boys?'

'It might be,' nodded Jess. 'We come to see if you got any cornflour.'

Farley smiled again, his head bobbing up and down. Billy Joe noticed that the girl didn't smile at all. He looked around to see if Duke Rixon and the gunmen were in tow, but there was no sign of them. He guessed they were too busy going around the township of tents, terrorising people, trying to force them to join the Cooperative.

'Indeed we do have cornflour,' said Farley. He indicated a large piece of slate propped up against the side of the wagon on which prices had been chalked.

Neither Jess nor Billy Joe could read properly, reading words was Shane's particular skill, but Shane had written down the words of what they wanted in a way that they could recognise them.

Jess's eyes narrowed as he saw that 'cornflour' had two prices against it – two dollars and six dollars.

'Why are there two prices for cornflour?' he demanded.

'One is the price for people who are in the Cooperative, and the other is for those who ain't,' smiled Farley. 'After all, it's only fair that people who join the Cooperative get something for their money, as well as protection.'

Billy Joe looked at the words and prices on the piece of slate and scoffed.

'Two dollars and six dollars!' he said derisively. 'A sack of cornflour only costs a dollar in Drygulch!'

'Well, you can always head over there to buy it, young fella,' said Farley. 'Ain't nothin' stoppin' you.' He paused, then added, ''Cept maybe someone steppin' in and grabbin' your claim while you're gone.'

'No one can do that,' said Jess. 'We got a claim, and so long as someone is here, that's our claim.'

'True,' agreed Farley, still smiling, 'but say two of you big boys had to go to Drygulch for something. Say, a sack of cornflour. That would leave the little 'uns on their own. Anything could happen to them then.'

'If it did, I'd kill the man who did it to 'em!' said Billy Joe angrily.

Farley studied Billy Joe thoughtfully, then he nodded. His smile had vanished.

'Yes, I believe you would, young fellow,' he said. 'But I guess that's the Injun in you.'

'I ain't no Injun!' Billy Joe burst out.

The fact was Billy Joe was half-Indian, half-Irish. His father had been an Irishman called John Ford, and the mother he'd never known a Comanche. Back home in Drygulch, Billy Joe had got used to people treating him just like any one of the gang. He didn't like Farley bringing up the colour of his skin now.

Farley turned to the girl.

'Sarah, put a note at the top of that slate. 'Every price, two dollars more for Injuns.'

'I ain't no Injun!' Billy Joe repeated, his voice rising in anger.

Farley shrugged.

'I hear what you say, boy, but you sure look Injun to me.' He turned to Jess. 'So, a sack of cornflour will be eight dollars to you. Unless this here Injun friend of yours quits and leaves, when the price will be six dollars.' He smiled. 'Now I guess you gonna be tellin' me you ain't got no money to pay upfront, so I'll make you the same offer I make everyone else – we'll put it on account and I'll charge you two cents a day until you pay it back. Just give Sarah your name and she'll make out the bill and do the paperwork, so it's all nice and legal.'

Jess shook his head. Inside he was boiling with rage, but he was determined not to give this greedy crook the pleasure of letting his anger show.

'We thank you for your offer, Mr Farley, but on reflection we'll go without the cornflour.'

Farley looked at Jess quizzically.

'You think eight dollars is too high a price?' he asked.

'Yep,' nodded Jess. Then he thought, *The hell with it! I'm gonna say what needs to be said to this crook*! 'But the real high price would be standin' here listenin' to you insult my friend and not sayin' nothin' back. As far as I'm concerned, you can stick your head in your cornflour and choke on it!' With that, he spat on the ground at Farley's feet, turned on his heel and walked away, calling, 'Come on, Billy Joe!'

Billy Joe hesitated, then he spat on the ground at Farley's feet as well, and hurried after Jess.

Farley shouted after them, 'For that, next time it'll cost you twenty dollars!'

Jess ignored him, and kept on walking. Billy Joe could see that his friend was fuming.

'What are we gonna do for flour, Jess?' he asked.

'We'll eat more fruit and rabbits instead,' muttered Jess. 'As soon as we get back, I'm goin' out huntin' with that dog; and he'd better find us somethin'.'

✸ ✸ ✸

That afternoon, as good as his word, Jess took Patch and a net and a knife, and went out hunting, leaving Billy Joe, Shane and Andy working the claim. Andy was furious, insisting that he should go too, as Patch was 'his' dog, but Jess was insistent; if Andy went he'd only scare the birds and animals they'd be hunting.

Andy remained sulky for the rest of the afternoon, but he brightened up when Jess and Patch returned with a brace of rabbits and a wood pigeon, which they skinned. Then Shane cooked the meat carefully over the fire and put some aside to be dried and kept for later. Dried meat wasn't nearly as tasty as fresh-cooked meat; it was hard and took a long time to chew; but if there was nothing else, it helped you feel less hungry.

As they settled down to sleep in the tent that night, Billy Joe felt good. Maybe they hadn't yet found any gold, but him and Jess had faced down Sam Farley, and they'd eaten a good meal. Today counted as Good Times.

CHAPTER 7

It was early afternoon of the next day when trouble arrived. Jess and Billy Joe were panning in the stream, with Robert Jackson panning on his side on the other bank. The sound of horses approaching at the top of the gulley made Jess and Billy Joe stop and look up. Farley's gunmen had pulled up and were getting down.

'Jackson, I got a message for you from Mr Farley,' called out Duke Rixon. He looked at Jess and Billy Joe and added, 'The same message goes for you too, boys.' Then he turned and shouted to the other prospectors working along both sides of the stream. 'And for any else of you who ain't yet signed up with Mr Farley!'

Billy Joe looked at the prospectors on the adjoining claims. The Bartletts had stopped panning and digging, and looked on warily. Next to them, Jasper Wade had also stopped and was watching. Further away, most of the prospectors ignored what was happening and just got on with their job; time was money, they didn't want to miss out on catching a nugget of gold because of some fool starting an argument.

'There ain't no message from Sam Farley that could hold any interest for me,' said Robert Jackson. 'And you can tell him so.'

With that, the young man spat on the ground and turned back to dipping his flat-bottomed pan in the shallow muddy waters.

Rixon scowled.

'I guess you ain't hearin' me right, Jackson,' he snorted. 'I said I got a message for you.'

'And I said I ain't interested in hearin' it,' retorted Robert, and he carried on panning, concentrating on the water slopping about in his pan.

Rixon glared at Robert, his face like thunder, and his hand dipped towards the handle of his gun in its holster, but one of the gunmen, a man called Jeb who had an ugly scar across his neck, made a low whistling sound, and as Rixon looked at him, Jeb shook his head. Billy Joe guessed Farley had told them he didn't want anyone shot at this stage. At least, not an unarmed person, and not in broad daylight.

Rixon moved his hand and slid down the steep ridge of rock and sandy soil. Robert obviously heard him coming, but he refused to turn and look at him, or even acknowledge Rixon's presence. *Brave, but stupid*, thought Billy Joe. *He's gonna get himself badly beaten*.

Rixon arrived behind Robert.

'Jackson,' he snapped. 'I'm talking to you!'

'Well I don't want to talk to you,' retorted Robert. 'So you can just get back on your horse and ride out of here and leave me alone.'

Rixon scowled again.

'No man turns his back on me,' he growled. 'That's a deliberate insult, and any man who insults me had better be ready to stand up for himself.'

At that, Robert turned and looked at Rixon.

'Stand up for himself?' he said, his tone mocking. 'Against six armed men? That the sort of odds you like, Rixon? Coward's odds?'

He's gone too far, groaned Billy Joe to himself. He could tell by the look of delight that had suddenly appeared on Rixon's face. He turned to the five men standing at the edge of the gulley.

'You hear that, boys?' he called. 'He called us cowards!' He turned and shouted, so all the other prospectors could hear. 'This man called me and my friend here cowards! Now you all know that sort of charge can't go unanswered. Now we ain't in the business of shootin' unarmed men, even though we got a right when someone calls us cowards to our face. But we do have a right to defend ourselves and our good name, right, Jeb?'

Jeb nodded.

'So why don't you come down here and explain that to young Jackson, here,' said Rixon. 'And you three, too.' To the remaining gunman he added, 'You better stay with the horses, Dan. We don't want any of this thievin' scum runnin' off with 'em.'

As four of the gunmen scrambled down the side of the gulley to join Rixon and Robert, Billy Joe whispered to Jess, 'You still think it's a bad idea to have a gun?'

'I do,' Jess whispered back. 'If Robert had waved a gun about, he'd be dead by now.'

'He'll be dead soon enough, the way this is goin',' muttered Billy Joe.

As they watched, Jeb struck the first blow, his huge fist catching Robert high on the forehead. Robert stumbled back and tried to regain his balance, but it was no good; the other men went into the attack with fists and boots, knocking Robert to the ground, and they carried on kicking him while Rixon stood and watched, a smug smile on his face.

Seeing this, Patch growled and was about to hurl himself at the gunmen, but Jess grabbed hold of the dog and held him back.

'You shoulda let Patch go for 'em!' urged Andy.

'And get himself shot?' asked Jess.

A cry went up from nearby.

'You're killing him!' Jane Bartlett shouted out in alarm, stepping forward only to be held back by her husband, Dan.

'No, ma'am, we're just teachin' him a lesson,' said Rixon. He took a look at Robert, who now lay semi-conscious on the ground, half in and half out of the water of the stream, his face bruised and bloody. 'OK, boys, that's enough!' he called.

Scrub gave one last kick which rocked Robert's body, and then the four gunmen stepped back, smiles of grim satisfaction on their faces.

Billy Joe looked at the young prospector lying on the ground. The fact that Robert gave little moans of pain was a good sign, as far as Billy Joe was concerned. It showed that Robert was alive, at least. But he'd been beaten very badly, and no one had lifted a finger to help him. No one except a woman and a foolhardy dog.

As the other gunmen clambered back up the slope to their horses, Rixon turned to make sure that his voice would carry all the way along both banks of the stream.

'Now listen here!' he yelled. 'From now on, everyone here is counted as being part of the Cooperative! Mr Farley wants fifty dollars from every claim. He's giving you two days to pay up.' Then he let out a nasty chuckle. 'I hear that some of you have got together and bought yourself some lady gunfighter, and the word is she'll be arriving any day. So here's the offer. You can pay fifty dollars now, or you can wait till your lady gunfighter's come and I've dealt with her. Once she's gone, the price goes up to a hundred dollars! So you've got your choice – fifty dollars now or a hundred dollars once this lady gunfighter of yours is carried out feet first!'

With that, Rixon hauled himself up the side of the gulley to his waiting horse.

'A lady gunfighter!' he chuckled. 'What's she use for a weapon? A broom?' Still laughing to himself, Rixon mounted his horse, then he and his gunmen rode away.

Jess and Shane immediately splashed their way across the shallow waters of the stream to where Robert Jackson lay, groaning. The Bartletts were also hurrying towards him. Jane Bartlett knelt down beside the injured man and used the hem of her dress to wipe the blood from his face while her son, Chris, held a cup of water to his bruised and bloodied lips.

'Here,' he said. 'Have some water. Might make you feel better!'

Robert mumbled something and shook his head, declining the drink.

Ed Bartlett came to join Jess and Shane. He hung his head sorrowfully.

'Looks like Farley's won,' he said. Apologetically, he added, 'I've got a wife and my two kids to think of. I can't afford to let what happened to Robert happen to them. I gotta pay.'

Jess nodded.

'I understand, Mr Bartlett,' he said.

'I'd advise you to pay as well, Jess,' said Bartlett.

Jess shook his head.

'No,' he said, 'I won't.'

Bartlett looked at Jess, then he sighed.

'I guess it ain't the same for you boys,' he said. 'You ain't got no family to think of.'

Jess looked across the stream to where Billy Joe and small Andy were standing, Andy with his arms around Patch's neck.

'Oh, we got family all right,' said Jess.

CHAPTER 8

The Bartletts did their best to treat Robert's injuries. Mrs Bartlett used some ointment she said she'd got from an Indian medicine man to paint on his bruises and rubbed some salve on his cuts. Jess, Shane and Billy Joe offered their help to the young prospector if he wanted it.

'We can look after your claim for a day or two,' said Jess. 'You're gonna need some time to get fit.'

Robert shook his head. He looked angry.

'They ain't gonna put me off my claim!' he said fiercely. 'This here's where my fortune's gonna be made, and I'm damned if I'm gonna give that up to Farley and Rixon and that pack of skunks!'

'You're still gonna need time,' insisted Jess. He saw Robert wince and said, 'If you ask me, I think one of your ribs is broke. That could be dangerous.'

'I don't need no time,' resisted Robert fiercely.

'Yeah, I reckon my rib is bust. But that don't worry me. I'll strap it up. I done it before.'

'You b-b-broke a rib before?' asked Shane.

Robert nodded, then stopped abruptly as the nodding made his head ache.

'I broke ribs and an arm and lots of things,' he said. 'Comes from workin' cattle. You get used to it. I know how to handle it.'

Footsteps behind them made them turn. It was Jimmy Flynn.

'I just heard what happened,' he said. Jimmy Flynn's claim was two miles further downstream. 'I hear there was a fight with Rixon and his boys.'

'It weren't no fight, Mr Flynn,' said Jess. 'It was a beatin' up. Five against one.'

Flynn shook his head sadly.

'I also heard the message Rixon brung from Farley. It seems most people are gonna pay.'

'Ed Bartlett says he is,' said Jess. 'Says he can't risk his family.'

Flynn nodded.

'What about you boys?' he asked.

'W-we ain't p-payin' F-Farley!' said Shane defiantly. 'Ain't th-that right, J-Jess?'

'It sure is,' Jess agreed quietly. 'OK, Billy Joe?'

Billy Joe hesitated, then he nodded.

'What about you, Mr Flynn?' asked Jess.

Flynn grinned.

'Hell, no. I ain't gonna pay. I'm far too mean! They can take me out in a box if they like, but I'm damned if I'm gonna pay that crook a bean!' He smiled. 'Anyway, I've already promised this Kitty Kelly my money for comin' here. I can't back out of that now. She might shoot me!' And he laughed.

Billy Joe looked thoughtful.

'So there's us, Mr Flynn, Robert Jackson and some lady against Farley and Rixon and his men.'

'Wh-when's this g-gunfighter l-lady comin', M-Mr F-Flynn?' asked Shane.

'She should be here tomorrow, about sundown,' said Flynn. 'I've told her to meet me at the bend of the stream, near the High Ridge. That way we'll find her without gettin' lost and missing each other.' He winked at the boys and lowered his voice and added, 'Just to make sure she gets here uninterrupted, I told everyone else she's arrivin' the day after tomorrow. So when that word spreads, like it will, it should give her some time before she has to face Rixon and his men.'

'You really think she can take on Rixon and five other gunmen, Mr Flynn?' asked Billy Joe doubtfully.

'If she can't, then I guess I've thrown away some good money,' said Flynn.

The next evening, after they'd finished work, Billy Joe and Shane went out to the High Ridge near where the stream bent. It was at the edge of the township of tents, about quarter of a mile from the gang's claim. Jimmy Flynn was already there when they arrived, brewing coffee over a small fire.

'After her long ride, I guess the lady will want somethin' to drink,' he said, stirring the thick brown liquid in the blackened can. He looked at Billy Joe and Shane. 'Where's Jess?' he asked.

'Back at our claim with Andy,' said Billy Joe. 'He said he thought all of us comin' might start tongues waggin' and cause unwelcome attention.'

'A-and it w-wouldn't d-do to leave the cl-claim unattended,' added Shane.

Flynn nodded.

'Jess has got a wise old head on those young shoulders of his,' he said. 'I got to say, I admire the way you boys look out for one another.'

The sound of a horse's hooves approaching caught their attention. Billy Joe turned and saw what looked at first sight to be a slim man on a horse. Then he realised it was a woman. And behind her, holding onto the saddle, sat a little girl.

'Here she is,' announced Flynn, and he got to his feet and took off his hat in greeting.

'Who's the little girl?' asked Billy Joe.

'Oh, that's her daughter,' said Flynn. 'I forgot to

mention her.' He smiled. 'But don't worry, we ain't got to pay any extra for the kid.'

Kitty Kelly pulled her horse to a halt and nodded to Flynn and Billy Joe. Billy Joe turned to see how Shane was reacting to this, and saw that his friend had retreated to the cover of a small scrappy tree. *Guess he's shy*, thought Billy Joe.

'Hi, Miz Kelly,' greeted Flynn. 'I'm Jimmy Flynn, the man who sent you the letter.'

'Good to meet you, Mr Flynn,' said Kelly, squinting in the sunshine.

'Hi, Miss Kelly.' Billy Joe lifted his hat. Well, it wasn't *his* hat as such, but Jess had given it to him and now Billy Joe wore it all the time.

Billy Joe watched as Kitty Kelly dismounted, before helping her young daughter get down. The little girl was about three or four years old, and dressed just like any little girl, with a dress that was all frills and lace with bows on it. Kitty Kelly was different. With her jeans, boots, jacket, and especially her gunbelt with the two guns hanging down by her side, she dressed like a man. Like a gunfighter. But her face was all woman.

She took off her hat and Billy Joe saw that she had red hair pulled back and tied and her skin was pale. There was something about her that was familiar, which puzzled Billy Joe, because he knew he'd never seen this woman before.

He walked over to Shane to tell him to stop being so rude, when he stopped. Shane was trembling, his face deathly white. Then suddenly the boy turned and hurried away.

'Hey!' Billy Joe called after him, but Shane just kept on walking.

'What in tarnation's wrong with him?' muttered Billy Joe.

He ambled after Shane, and caught up with his friend just as Shane got back to their tent. Billy Joe was surprised to see him hurry inside and pull down the flap.

Jess and Andy were just a few paces away, breaking thin sticks of wood to use as kindling for their fire. Jess frowned as he saw Billy Joe arrive.

'Was that Shane who went in the tent just now?' he asked, puzzled.

'Sure was,' nodded Billy Joe.

'What's up with him?' demanded Jess.

'Maybe he got scared by someone,' Andy piped up. 'Some gunman.'

'Well we just saw a gunman right enough,' agreed Billy Joe. 'Only she ain't a gunman. She's a gunwoman.'

'Kitty Kelly's here?' asked Jess.

'Yes,' nodded Billy Joe.

'Wow!' exclaimed Andy excitedly. 'Where is she? I gotta see her! Is she ugly? Any woman who fights has got to be ugly. I bet she's got a bashed-in face!'

'You'd lose your bet,' Billy Joe said. 'She's a real good-lookin' woman. Got her hair all tied back proper, like any woman you'd see on the street or goin' to church. Got a proper little girl with her as well. It's her daughter.' He frowned. 'I can't see why the look of her would scare Shane so.'

'Guess we'd better ask him,' said Jess.

Jess walked towards the tent, Billy Joe and Andy following him, and Patch following them. When Jess lifted the flap of the tent they could see Shane sitting on the ground clasping his knees, his face still deathly white.

'What's the matter, Shane?' asked Jess. 'You run in here like a ghost was after you.'

'Th-that woman,' stammered Shane.

'Kitty Kelly?' asked Jess.

Shane nodded.

'What about her?' asked Jess. 'You know her?'

Again Shane nodded, and now the boys could see the start of tears in his eyes.

'Sh-sh-she's my m-mother,' he said.

Jess and Billy Joe exchanged stunned looks.

Andy let out a chuckle of delight.

'Wow!' he said. 'A gunfighter for a mother! Wow!'

'Ssh, Andy!' ordered Jess sharply. He cast a look at Shane, then said to Andy, 'Maybe you'd better take Patch out somewhere, while me and Shane talk.'

'N-no,' said Shane. 'A-Andy has a right to hear

th-this. H-he's one of us.'

Jess and Billy Joe moved further inside the tent and sat down near to Shane. Andy sat down by the entrance, Patch thumping down on the ground beside him, his warm brown eyes looking at Shane like he knew something was wrong.

'I th-thought she was d-dead,' said Shane, his voice still showing his shock.

And then he told the others his story, and for the first time, Billy Joe heard about how Shane had come to join the gang.

Shane and his older brother Pete had lived in a small town with their father, Henry Hogan, and their mother, Kitty. Henry Hogan was a violent man, drunk or sober, who seemed to take delight in beating up his wife and sons. As the older brother, Pete did his best to protect Shane from their father's rages and brutality, but time and time again Henry Hogan battered both Shane and Pete. It had been Henry Hogan who'd broken Shane's nose. He'd also broken Pete's arm, and knocked out his teeth.

Things came to a head after Kitty Hogan gave birth to their new child, a baby girl, Emma. Henry Hogan's rages became worse after the arrival of his daughter, and Shane knew that his mother worried that Hogan might harm the baby, possibly even kill her. One day, Kitty took Emma and ran away. At the time, Shane had been six years old, and Pete nine.

When he discovered that his wife had run off, Henry Hogan took a gun and a whip and set off after her. Both Pete and Shane were sure he'd kill them both when he caught up with them.

It was Pete who took action. Pete guessed that when Henry Hogan came back, he would kill Pete and Shane as well. So he packed clothes for himself and his brother, and then the two boys ran away.

Determined that Hogan wouldn't find them, Pete kept them on the move at first – one night here, one night there. Each day a new direction – one day south, the next day east – and never told anyone their name was Hogan, just in case word got back to their father.

After a year of living like this, they arrived at the shack in Drygulch, where they met up with Jess. They hadn't told Jess their background, and they hadn't asked for his.

After a further year with no word of Henry Hogan, Shane and Pete had hoped that was the end of it.

'You never thought about your ma and sister?' asked Billy Joe.

'We r-reckoned he m-must've k-killed 'em,' said Shane. 'M-Ma couldn't have g-got f-far b-before Pa set out after her, and we kn-knew what s-sort of m-man he was.'

They fell silent.

'You sure it's your ma?' asked Andy. 'This woman's name is Kelly.'

'No law against changin' your name,' said Billy Joe. 'Especially if people are lookin' for you.'

'You reckon your pa's still lookin' for her?' asked Jess.

'That d-don't s-seem likely,' admitted Shane. 'Not with her w-walkin' around like th-this.'

They fell silent again, and then Jess said, 'I guess the only way to find out is to ask her.'

CHAPTER 9

Shane stood and watched as Kitty Kelly and the little girl finished putting up their tent. There was no shortage of people standing around offering to help, or just standing and gawking. Men and women and children stood and watched as if they'd never seen anything like her before. And the truth was, most of them hadn't. A woman who earned her living as a gunfighter was a rarity.

It had been three years since Shane had last seen her, and the person here was a vastly different individual to the mother he'd known. That woman had suffered beatings and kicks and had never fought back. That woman had been a victim. This one here, now, was strong-willed and not afraid of anything. It was hard to think that she was the same person.

He looked at the little girl, at his sister, Em. She was busy unwrapping a bedroll, and taking things out and putting them in the tent. The last time Shane had seen Em she'd just been a baby, not even talking properly and still crawling.

Shane waited until the men and women stopped their staring and drifted away, leaving Kitty Kelly to finish making camp. As the last woman moved off, Shane approached.

The woman seemed unaware of him, she was busy checking something in her saddle bag. Shane opened his mouth to speak, but no words came. He tried again, but again he'd been struck dumb. Tears of frustration sprang into his eyes. He bit his lip, and then tried again, forcing out that one word: 'M-Ma!'

It was as if some invisible person had come up and punched Kelly. At the sound, she swung round, her mouth open, shocked, her eyes going wide as she looked at Shane. And then she burst out, 'Shane?!'

Then Shane was running towards her as she dropped to her knees, her arms outstretched, and the boy ran into her arms and was lost in a big hug that nearly crushed him. It was as if all those years of absence and loss had vanished in that one hug.

'Oh, Shane!' said Kelly. 'I thought you were dead! I thought I'd never see you again!'

She pushed back her son at arm's length and studied him. Shane could see the tears in her eyes, and could feel his own eyes welling up. Then Kelly pulled him to her and folded him up in her arms again.

'Who's this, Ma?' said a small, puzzled voice.

Kelly released Shane, a big smile spread right across her face, and looked at the little girl who'd come up to them.

'Em,' she said proudly, 'come and say hello to your brother!'

The little girl came up to Shane and looked at him thoughtfully.

'Are you really my brother?' she asked.

Shane nodded.

'Y-yes,' he said. 'M-my n-name's Shane.'

'Where's Pete?' asked Kelly, her eyes scanning the camp for the sight of her older son.

'H-he's dead,' said Shane.

Kelly stared at him, stunned.

'Dead?'

The pain on Kitty Kelly's face at learning she'd found one son, only to know she'd lost the other, was unbearable. She seemed to sag, as if she was about to fall. Then she threw her arms around Shane again.

'Let's go in our tent, son,' she said. 'We got a lot of catchin' up to do.'

✸ ✸ ✸

Kelly spread a tarpaulin on the earth inside the tent so they could sit without getting damp from the moist ground.

'You want me to make us somethin' to eat?' she asked Shane.

Shane shook his head.

'I w-want to kn-know what happened to Pa,' he said. 'Wh-when m-me an' P-Pete last saw h-him he w-was comin' a-after you with a wh-whip an' a g-gun.'

Kelly nodded soberly.

'And he caught up with us in a little town called Brushwood,' she said. 'He pointed a gun at us. Said he was gonna shoot Em right in front of me to teach me a lesson so I'd never go runnin' off again.' She sighed. 'I don't know what came over me. Till that day I'd been afraid of him. He was bigger than me and stronger than me. But when I saw him pointin' that gun at Em somethin' snapped inside me. I grabbed at the gun and we struggled, and next thing the gun went off and he was dead.

'That first day I was in a panic. I kept expectin' a Sheriff or someone to come lookin' for me. But no one did.

'The next day, I went straight home to find you. I just wanted to put my arms around both of you and for us to be a family again, a proper family this time. But when I got back there was no sign of you or Pete. Someone told me they'd seen you sneakin' off with bedrolls, so I guessed you'd run away. I started lookin' for you right off, but I couldn't pick up your trail.'

'Th-that's c-cos Pete made s-sure no one would

f-find us. He d-didn't want P-Pa catchin' up with us.'

Kelly nodded.

'That sounds like my son,' she agreed, tears filling her eyes again. 'I stayed home for a while, hopin' that maybe you'd both come back. But you didn't. Then questions started bein' asked about what had happened to Henry Hogan. Most people said he'd run off, but there were reports that he'd got shot in Brushwood by a woman.

'So I decided it was time to move on and start life fresh. I went back to my old name, which was Kelly. An' all the time I kept lookin' for you boys. Everywhere I went I asked about two boys, but always the answer was "no".'

'How d-did you g-get to b-be a gunfighter?' asked Shane.

Kelly shrugged.

'I just sort of grew into it,' she said. 'After what had happened with your pa beatin' me and threatenin' to kill Em, I vowed I'd never let myself be in that position ever again. So I started practisin' with a gun to make sure I could defend myself.' She gave a shy smile. 'I found I was good at it. I could shoot straight and accurate. And then I got quick.' She laughed at the memories. 'Em and me were in this town where this man was takin' out his gun an' shootin' at this unarmed man and his wife and family for fun. Tryin' to make 'em dance in the street. He'd put his gun back in his holster to make them think it was over, then he'd pull it out and start shootin' at 'em again. I told him to stop. He got angry and went to pull his gun on me, but I beat him to it.' She chuckled. 'I can still see the look on his face as he found himself looking at the gun in my hand, and his hadn't even cleared the holster. I made him apologise to the man and his family, and then advised him to get on his way. Which he did.' She smiled. 'That's what got me my reputation, and I didn't even have to fire a shot.'

'B-but y-you have s-since?' asked Shane.

'Fired a shot?' asked his mother.

Shane nodded.

Kelly sighed. 'Yes, I'm afraid to say I have. I've killed six men, all in fair fights. I'm not proud of it, but they were killers every one. Dangerous to other folk, innocent folk. And makin' a livin' isn't easy for a woman out West, especially when you've got a young daughter to bring up. Being a gun for hire pays better than takin' in sewing.'

Shane fell silent, then finally he asked the question that had haunted him ever since his mother had left all that time ago. 'W-why d-didn't you t-take us with you w-when you r-ran off?'

Kelly dropped her eyes from his gaze.

'I couldn't take all of you,' she said, her voice so low Shane had to strain to hear what she was saying. 'I knew if I had any chance of gettin' away, I could only take one. I chose Em.' She looked up at him, and now Shane saw that tears were rolling down her cheeks. 'It was the hardest thing I've ever had to do, Shane, to leave you and Pete. But I knew that if I left Em, she was as good as dead with that evil animal. I hoped you and Pete, bein' older, might have more of a chance of makin' it without me.' She dropped her head again. 'I'm sorry.'

'Th-that's OK,' said Shane. He looked across at his young sister, playing with her rag doll on the tarpaulin. 'It w-was the r-right th-thing to do.'

Kelly shook her head.

'No,' she said, 'it wasn't. I should've killed him instead of runnin' off, then we could've been together as a family, and maybe Pete would still be alive.'

Shane looked at his mother, at the tears pouring down her face, and suddenly he was overcome with everything – with the pain of his mother leaving; with Pete being shot dead; but mostly now at the fact he was with his mother and sister again. And then Shane was crying too, and he felt his mother's arms envelop him.

'It's OK. Ma's here, son,' she whispered. 'And I ain't gonna lose you again!'

CHAPTER 10

Billy Joe, Jess and Andy sluiced themselves in the water from the stream. It was supposed to get them clean after a hard day's work, before they settled down for supper, but Billy Joe noticed that often they were dirtier after they'd been in the water than they had been before they washed. He guessed it was all the silt that built up in the water from the workings upstream from their claim.

They got back to their tent and Jess set to work building a fire for cooking and drying off their clothes. Andy took Patch in search of small sticks and brushwood to use for kindling. Billy Joe just lay down on the ground and looked at the sky, his body aching. This gold-mining sure was back-breaking hard work. And they hadn't even found so much as a pinch of gold dust.

'Hi, boys!'

Billy Joe sat up and found himself looking up into the face of Kitty Kelly. Next to her, Shane was smiling broadly and holding the hand of the little girl, Em.

'Th-this is my m-ma!' said Shane proudly.

'Yeah,' nodded Billy Joe. 'We met.'

'Pleased to meet you, Miz Kelly,' smiled Jess politely.

'I just wanted to come over and meet you and say thank you for looking after Shane the way you have,' said Kelly.

'I l-look after th-them as w-well!' protested Shane indignantly.

'Of course you do,' nodded Kelly, a twinkle in her eye.

'Would you care to join us, ma'am?' asked Jess. 'As soon as Andy gets back with the kindling we'll have a real good fire goin'.'

'Thanks, but no,' smiled Kelly. 'I want to go and meet the rest of the people I've been hired to protect.'

'That won't take much time,' said Billy Joe. 'It's just us, Mr Flynn, Robert and Barnardo. The rest of 'em have signed up with Farley.'

'Then I'll go see those gentlemen you mentioned,' said Kelly. 'Mr Flynn has suggested I meet up with him, and he'll show me around.' She indicated her little daughter. 'While I do that, Shane has said he'll look after little Em here.'

'Sh-she's my s-sister!' Shane said proudly, squeezing Em's hand.

'Would that be all right with the rest of you?' asked Kelly.

Billy Joe wanted to point out that they weren't nursemaids. But then he remembered that Kitty Kelly was supposed to be a fast gunfighter, and it didn't do to upset gunfighters. And anyway, Jess had already cut in with, 'It will be our pleasure, ma'am.'

'I s-said we c-could l-look after Em to-tomorrow, as well,' smiled Shane.

Billy Joe's heart sank. He wasn't keen on playing nursemaid to no one. Still, seeing the smile it brought to Shane's face, it was a small price to pay. Shane had had enough pain in his young life. It was about time something good happened to him, and having his ma and his baby sister turn up was *really* good. Billy Joe hoped it kept being good for Shane, and didn't go bad, like so many things seemed to do.

Just then, Andy and Patch arrived back. Andy was carrying a bundle of small twigs and little bits of brush, and Patch carried some brushwood in his mouth.

'We found stuff, Jess!' he said.

'Th-this here's Andy!' introduced Shane. To Andy, he said, 'Th-is is my s-sister, Em. She's g-gonna be with us tomorrow.'

'Great,' beamed Andy. 'I can teach her how to dig for gold! It's fun!'

'Em's gonna stay with us now for a bit, while Miz Kelly goes to meet people,' added Jess.

'She can sit with me and Patch,' announced Andy. 'Do you like dogs?' he asked Em.

'Some,' said Em. 'I don't like dogs that bite.'

'Patch don't bite,' said Andy. 'Except for bad people. He's a good dog. Come here and say hello, Patch.'

Andy dropped his brushwood and twigs on the floor and walked over to Em, Patch following, tongue lolling and eyes shining.

'You can stroke him,' said Andy. 'He won't hurt you.'

Cautiously, Em put out a hand and patted Patch very gently. Patch, always keen for any sign of affection, rolled on his back, legs in the air. Immediately, Andy dropped down and rubbed Patch's belly, then grabbed the dog's ears and tugged at them.

'You'll hurt him,' said Em, concerned.

'No, he likes it!' chattered Andy. 'So long as you don't tug too hard.'

Kelly smiled.

'Well, everything seems safe enough here,' she said. 'I guess I'll go and talk with Mr Flynn. See you in a moment, Em.'

But Em was busy playing with Andy and Patch, all three of them rolling over on the ground in a friendly wrestling match.

Billy Joe looked at them and gave a rueful sigh.

'Kids!' he said.

CHAPTER 11

The next morning the boys were up early. Shane was especially excited.

'R-remember we g-gotta m-make sure we t-take g-good care of Em,' he insisted. 'So no pl-playin' tr-tricks on her, Andy,' he warned.

'Why would I do that?' demanded Andy as he pulled on his boots.

'B-because that's what you d-do,' Shane said.

'Don't worry, Shane,' Jess assured him. 'We'll keep her safe.'

Not like her mother, said Billy Joe silently to himself. *Once Rixon finds out she's here, he's going to come gunning for her. He'll shoot her dead right in front of everyone, just to make an example of her, so that everyone knows they must either pay up or die. Sure, Kitty Kelly looked the part, with her guns slung low on her hips, but how would she fare against a killer like Rixon. And not just Rixon, there would be another five gunmen with him. Six gunmen against one woman*. He kicked himself mentally for having agreed to it in the first place. This wasn't a good idea. As soon as Rixon and his men turned up and killed Kitty Kelly, the boys should pack up and head back to Drygulch and forget about this gold foolishness. Abbey Vernon had been right. Though now there would be the problem of what to do about Shane's little sister, Em. If it was up to Billy Joe, he'd put her in an orphanage, but he knew already that Shane would want the gang to look after her. And Jess would agree, because Jess always took in strays who needed help. Like Patch, the dog. Like Shane and Pete and Andy. *And like me*, he thought ruefully.

The boys were outside their tent, making their morning coffee, when Kitty Kelly arrived, bringing her little daughter by the hand.

'M-morning, M-Ma!' piped up Shane, a big smile on his face, and Billy Joe's heart sank. This was going to be worse than he thought. First, Shane had seen his brother, Pete, gunned down right before his eyes, and now he was going to see his ma go the same way.

'This is a bad idea,' he muttered.

'What is?' asked Jess.

Billy Joe looked up at Jess, and then at the others, uncomfortable. He hadn't intended to say it out loud.

'Hiring me?' asked Kelly.

Billy Joe hesitated, then he nodded.

'Why?' Shane demanded angrily, leaping to his mother's defence. 'B-because she's a w-woman?'

'No, because she's your ma,' said Billy Joe, annoyed. He didn't judge folk by how they looked. 'If she gets killed, you'll go to pieces.'

'First I got to get killed,' said Kelly. 'And I ain't intendin' to do that any time soon.'

'You may not be intendin' it, but you're gonna be up against six gunmen,' insisted Billy Joe. 'Don't that make you think?'

'Billy Joe, she's our guest,' said Jess, a tone of reprimand in his voice. 'And I don't think she'd be here if she hadn't thought about it.'

Kelly smiled.

'Thank you, Jess,' she said, 'And you're quite right. I always think about what I'm doin'. That's how I've managed to stay alive.' Then her tone changed, and she said, 'Anyway I think it's a bit too late for me to change my mind.'

The boys saw that Kelly was looking at something behind them. They turned and Billy Joe froze to the spot, a lump of fear in his throat. Duke Rixon and his five gunmen were pushing their way through the crowded tents on horseback, trampling over people's camps. There was no mistaking the look of hard determination on their faces. Prospectors backed away from them as they came nearer the boys' tent, and Kitty Kelly.

'Shane, why don't you take your sister along to your claim,' murmured Kelly. 'And maybe Andy would like to go with you.'

'No way!' exclaimed Andy indignantly. 'I wanna see you stop these bad men!'

I'd like to see that too, thought Billy Joe unhappily, but he couldn't see how it was going to happen.

Rixon and his men pulled up their horses, and Rixon gave a cold smile.

'So,' he said. 'I guess you must be the famous Kitty Kelly, the fastest draw in the West.'

At this, the five men with him snickered.

Rixon gestured at the guns hanging down from Kitty Kelly's gunbelt.

'Why don't you show me how fast you are,' he grinned.

'Now why should I waste my time doing a fool thing like that?' asked Kelly, also smiling, but there was no humour in the smile.

'Because I hear you're fast,' said Rixon. 'Now it could be just some story that's been spread, because I never heard of no one near as fast as me. Leastways a woman.'

'Then I guess you ain't met many people,' said Kelly. 'But then, it could be people don't wanna meet you, cos you sure is one of the ugliest and most objectionable people I ever seen.'

She was still smiling. Rixon had stopped smiling.

'What you say?' he demanded.

74

'Of course,' continued Kelly, 'there is one way to find out how fast I am, and that's to reach for that gun of yours.'

Rixon's face hardened.

'Lady,' he snapped, 'if I draw my gun, I use it.'

'Well, ain't that interestin',' shrugged Kelly. 'You sure do *talk* good gunplay. You ever actually ever *used* it?'

'Why you –' snarled Rixon, and his hand snatched down fast for his gun. Then he stopped. Kelly had both guns in her hands and was pointing one at Rixon with the other moving to cover his men.

Kelly was no longer smiling.

'Guess you ain't as fast as you thought you were,' she said.

The other gunmen were looking at her, then at Rixon, with astonishment clear on their faces.

Kelly addressed them.

'If any of you others are thinkin' of tryin' anythin', don't,' she said. 'I'm as good with my left hand as I am with my right. And it ain't my wish to waste good money on bullets for you bunch. But I will if I have to.'

Suddenly Billy Joe saw that the gunman at the back, Scrub, the farthest from Kelly's line of sight, was pulling his gun from his holster.

'Kelly!' he yelled in warning, but there was no need. The gun in Kelly's left hand shot flame and the gunman gave a yell of pain and fell off his horse. He lay on the ground clutching his arm and moaning. Rixon and the others looked at him lying there, shocked.

'Don't worry, he ain't dead,' said Kelly dismissively. 'If he was he wouldn't be making that awful racket.' She gestured at them with both her guns. 'Pick him up and take him out of here. But before you leave, I'm impoundin' your guns.'

Rixon stared at her, shock on his face.

'You're *what*?' he demanded.

'Impounding,' she said. 'It's a big word, so I'll make it simple. It means I'm taking your guns off you to make sure you don't come back and shoot me, or any of the people I'm here to protect, in the back.'

The gunman with the scar on his neck, Jeb, looked at Rixon in horror.

'She can't do that, can she, Duke?' he demanded.

'I'm the one holdin' the gun. I can do what I want,' Kelly snapped. 'When I've decided I can trust you, I'll give 'em back.' She turned to Jess, Billy Joe and Shane. 'You boys want to do me a favour and collect up their guns?'

Shane grinned.

'I s-sure do,' he chuckled.

Kelly turned back to Rixon and the four gunmen still sitting on their horses. 'Right, get your hands in the air. These boy are gonna come round and take your guns. You make any sort of move and I'll shoot you dead.' With that, she nodded at the three boys. 'Go get 'em.'

Jess and Shane moved forwards swiftly and began to take the gunmen's pistols from their holsters. Billy Joe went to the fallen Scrub, who was still lying on the ground moaning. Billy Joe lifted out his pistol and looked down at the groaning man.

'My Irish pa told me never to upset a woman with red hair. Guess you learned that the hard way.'

The three boys returned to where Kelly was standing, guns still ready for use.

'OK,' said Kelly to Rixon and his men, 'you can go. And if you come back looking for revenge, I'll kill you. That's a promise.'

'This ain't over!' snarled Rixon.

'I agree,' nodded Kelly. 'It's over when I say it is, and that'll be when you leave these people in peace.'

Rixon didn't reply, he just sat on his horse glaring at the gunfighter. Then he spat on the ground, aiming as near to Kelly's feet as he could. Kelly didn't move or react, she stood there impassively with her guns trained on the men.

Rixon scowled and turned his horse, and then rode off, shouting, 'Pick up Scrub!' at the others.

The other gunmen hesitated, then dismonted and lifted Scrub up, helping him onto his horse. The boys saw Scrub wince in pain and guessed the bullet had broken his arm. With his good hand Scrub took hold of the reins, then the other gunmen got back on their horses and rode away after the departing Rixon.

'Wow!' said Andy. He looked at Kelly admiringly. 'You're the best gunman I ever saw!'

Kelly smiled and pushed her pistols back in their holsters.

'Glad you think so, Andy,' she said. 'Well, I don't think they'll be back any time soon, so I guess there's time for me to cook some breakfast for me and Em. What do you reckon, Em?'

'Yes!' nodded Em, completely unmoved by seeing her mother face down six men. Turning to Andy, she said, 'We got ham! And Ma got some eggs as we was comin' in yesterday!'

'I c-an c-cook h-ham and eggs!' Shane spoke up.

Kelly looked her son, surprised.

'You sure?' she asked.

'Y-yes,' nodded Shane.

'He's a good cook, ma'am,' agreed Jess.

'And we can eat with you as well, can't we!' said Andy enthusiastically.

'No,' said Jess firmly.

Andy looked crestfallen.

'Why not?'

'Because we got things to do.' Jess turned to Kelly and Shane. 'We'll see you all later.'

'We sure will,' nodded Kelly. Then she stopped. 'Oh, Billy Joe –'

Billy Joe looked at her, curious.

She smiled. 'Thanks for callin' out to warn me when

that gunman drew.'

'You didn't need it,' said Billy Joe. 'You already had him covered.'

'Yeah, but I mightn't have,' said Kelly. 'Thanks.'

With that, she took Em by the hand, then, with Shane walking beside them, they headed for their tent.

Andy scowled. 'Why can't we go eat with 'em?' he demanded.

'Family time,' murmured Billy Joe with a smile.

CHAPTER 12

Word about the confrontation between Kitty Kelly and Duke Rixon and his men spread among the prospectors like wildfire. By mid-afternoon, Kitty Kelly was being welcomed wherever she went, and there was no shortage of people offering to watch over Em for her while the gunfighter went about her business. Kelly, however, was happy to say that looking after her daughter was well taken care of.

Em seemed very happy to be left with the gang. While Billy Joe and Jess panned for gold in the stream, Shane kept Em and Andy with him higher up the gulley, where they scratched and dug at the soil, looking out for anything bright and shiny that might be gold.

The hot sun shone down on them, but it didn't seem to bother Em. She had the tanned skin of someone who was used to living outside. Unlike her mother, who had one of the palest faces Billy Joe had ever seen.

All the time they worked, Billy Joe kept half an eye out for Rixon and his men, but by late-afternoon there was still no sign of them. Instead, Jimmy Flynn arrived at their claim.

'Hi, boys!' called Flynn with a friendly wave.

Shane and Andy stopped working and waved back at him.

'Any luck, Mr Flynn?' asked Jess.

Flynn shook his head ruefully. 'If there's gold, it sure is keepin' itself well hidden from me. Though I hear the Pattersons have found a couple of nuggets further upstream.'

'Gold!' yelled Andy excitedly. 'They found gold! Come on, Shane! There *is* gold here!'

And he set back to work with renewed energy, digging and scratching at the soil.

Flynn watched Andy working and shook his head.

'There's gold sure enough,' he sighed. 'The question is, is there enough to make it worth a man breakin' his back?' He stood there, and Jess and Billy Joe could see there was something troubling him. Finally, he said, 'Jess, can I talk to you a moment?'

'Sure, Mr Flynn,' nodded Jess. He stopped panning and wiped the wet palms of his hands on his jacket.

'You too, Billy Joe, if you don't mind,' added Flynn. He turned to Shane and Andy and said to them with a smile, 'Don't take offence, you youngsters, but it looks to me like you got enough to do there with takin' care of that little girl.'

'N-none t-taken, Mr F-Flynn,' said Shane, though Billy Joe was sure that Shane felt disappointed at being left out.

Andy, on the other hand, had no qualms about making his protest at being described as a youngster.

'I ain't no little 'un!' he protested.

'Andy, all Mr Flynn means is that you and Shane are needed to take care of Em, and also see that the diggin' keeps goin',' said Jess. 'Right now, those are two big important jobs.'

'I-I'll look after 'em,' Shane assured them, and he called Andy over to join him and Em at a patch of ground they were raking over.

Jess and Billy Joe joined Jimmy Flynn. They both noticed that the old prospector looked worried.

'What's the matter, Mr Flynn?' asked Jess. 'I'd a thought you'd a bin pleased with the way Kitty Kelly handled Rixon and his men.'

'I know I should be, but I ain't. Somethin's troublin' me,' admitted Flynn.

'What?' asked Billy Joe, puzzled. 'Everyone's seen that Rixon and his men ain't no match for Kitty Kelly, not in speed or shootin' straight. I bet a lot of people are sayin' they ain't gonna pay Farley for protection now after all.'

'That's right,' agreed Flynn with a nod. He sighed. 'The thing is, boys, I'm old, I seen a lot, and one thing I know, people like Sam Farley and Duke Rixon don't like bein' shown up that way. They especially don't like it when it costs them money. Like you say, a lot of people are now sayin' they won't pay Farley for joinin' his Cooperative, they'd rather pay money to Kitty Kelly to protect them.'

Billy Joe grinned.

'That's great!' he said. 'Now all it needs is someone to open up a store that sells stuff cheaper than Sam Farley and he's finished. Him and his men will just have to pack up and sneak off.'

Flynn shook his head sadly.

'That ain't likely to happen any time soon, Billy Joe,' he said. 'Farley has got too much invested here. Lots of people owe him money. He's countin' on one of them strikin' gold. That's all he needs. One good gold strike and he gets his money back, and a lot more besides. A man like that ain't just gonna walk away.'

'So what d'you think he's gonna do?' asked Jess.

'I think he's gonna try somethin',' murmured Flynn. 'Somethin' sneaky and underhand to get rid of Kitty Kelly.'

'Shoot her in the back, like he did John Vernon?' asked Billy Joe.

'Maybe, but she ain't like John Vernon. She's fast with a gun, and she's aware of what's goin' on. I seen the way she moves around, like she's got eyes and ears all over her!'

'That's how she's stayed alive this far,' nodded Jess.

'Right,' agreed Flynn. 'Now any normal gunman would see that and accept it and leave her alone. But Duke Rixon ain't normal. There's something unstable about him. I seen hotheads before, and he's one.'

Billy Joe and Jess nodded.

'We got him pegged like that as well, Mr Flynn,' said Jess.

'He's trigger-happy,' added Billy Joe.

'So what worries me is what Rixon will do about Kitty Kelly, now he knows he can't beat her face to face in the open.'

Jess looked thoughtful.

'I guess it's up to us to try and find out,' he said. 'What d'you think, Billy Joe?'

Billy Joe nodded.

'I reckon you're right, Jess.' He gave a rueful smile. 'Guess it better be me.'

Jess looked at Billy Joe and laughed.

'You ain't gonna try and tell me you're better at it cos you is half-Injun, are you, Billy Joe?' he chuckled.

Billy Joe smiled and shook his head.

'No,' he said. 'It's just that I'm sneakier. And we need you to be on the claim lookin' after the others.'

Jimmy Flynn looked from one to the other.

'What in tarnation are you boys talkin' about?'

he asked, puzzled

'What you was just talkin' about, Mr Flynn,' said Jess. 'Findin' out what sneaky tricks Farley and his men have got in mind for Kitty Kelly.'

'Tonight when it gets dark I'll go to Farley's wagons and see if I can hear what him and Rixon is plannin',' said Billy Joe.

Flynn looked at the two boys thoughtfully, weighing up their plan.

'That's a good thought,' he agreed, 'but Farley and Rixon could be plannin' somethin' right now.

Billy Joe and Jess shook their heads.

'Too many people around,' said Jess. 'While the store wagon's open Farley will be makin' money. He won't want to spend time talkin' about what to do. And especially when people can hear what he's thinkin' of doin'.'

Jimmy Flynn nodded, impressed by the boy's logic.

'That makes sense, Jess,' he agreed. 'But I didn't expect you boys to put yourselves in any danger. Farley and Rixon are dangerous men. If they catch you, Billy Joe, you being a boy ain't gonna make no difference to what they do to you.'

'I know that,' nodded Billy Joe. 'That's why I'm gonna make real sure I don't get caught.'

CHAPTER 13

When the sun began to go down and work ended for the day, Kitty Kelly came to the boys' tent. Andy was playing a pat-a-cake game with Em, the two slapping the palms of their hands against one another.

'D-don't be t-too rough, Andy,' warned Shane. 'Sh-she's only l-little.'

'I ain't bein' too rough,' said Andy defensively. 'And she's enjoyin' it.'

Em certainly appeared to be. She was laughing as she slapped her hand against Andy's and laughing even more as he missed hers; deliberately, Billy Joe suspected.

Patch lay on the ground nearby and watched, his tongue hanging out of his mouth, fascinated by this odd game.

'Seems a pity to break things up when you're having so much fun,' smiled Kelly.

'You're welcome to come and join us, ma'am,' said Jess, gesturing at the tarpaulin on the ground. 'We're just about to start makin' our supper.'

'With no cornbread!' moaned Andy.

'We'll have cornbread later, Andy,' promised Jess.

'Thanks for the offer, Jess,' nodded Kelly, 'but Em is gonna need her sleep. So my plan is to feed us and then put her to bed.' She smiled at her son. 'Would you like to come too, Shane?'

The boy's face lit up.

'I s-sure would!' he said, and started to get up, but Jess stopped him.

'Before he does, Miz Kelly, d'you mind if we have a word with him?' he asked.

Kelly looked at Jess in surprise, then shook her head.

'Not at all,' she said.

'It won't take but a minute,' Jess went on. 'It's gang stuff. Nothin' special.'

Kelly smiled.

'That's fine,' she said. 'I'll take Em and give her a wash. Then I'll see you in a while, Shane.'

'You b-bet!' he grinned.

'Come on, Em!' said Kelly. When she saw that the little girl looked reluctant to stop playing with Andy and Patch, she added, 'You can play here again tomorrow. That's a promise.'

Em smiled and got up, patted Patch, who licked her

face, and then ran to her mother. Kitty Kelly took Em by the hand, and the two walked off.

Billy Joe watched them go, looking at the guns hanging in their holsters by Kelly's sides. *That's some great woman*, he thought. *Beautiful, a real good loving Ma, and as deadly with those pistols as any gunman he'd ever seen. Shane was lucky to have found her again.*

'W-what's up, Jess?' Shane said, turning to Jess, a look of concern on his face.

Jess checked to make sure that no one was near enough to overhear them, then he told Shane what they were planning – that Billy Joe was going to Farley's wagons that night to try and find out what Farley and Rixon had planned for Kitty Kelly.

'We thought it was only right you should know, Shane, on account of her bein' your ma. We don't want to worry you.' He turned to Andy. 'And we thought you should know, Andy, cos you're part of this gang and you got a right to know what's happenin'.'

'Plus we don't want you goin' runnin' around tonight shoutin' out wonderin' where Billy Joe is,' added Billy Joe pointedly.

'I wouldn't!' protested Andy.

'Yes, you would,' insisted Billy Joe.

'I w-want t-to go t-too,' said Shane firmly. 'L-like you s-said, she's my ma. If F-Farley an' R-Rixon are plannin' on killin' her, I g-got a right to kn-know what it is so I can st-stop it.'

'We never said anythin' about Farley killin' your ma,' said Jess. 'Just about doin' somethin' to stop her helpin' us.'

'And th-that means k-killin' her,' said Shane. 'Ain't n-no other way they c-can do it.'

Billy Joe looked at Jess.

'Shane's right, Jess,' he said. 'She's a gunfighter, and we already seen she ain't the type to run away.'

Jess thought it over, then nodded.

'OK,' he said. 'It might be better if there's two of you.' Then he shot a firm look at Shane and added, 'But don't you go tellin' your ma about this. We're doin' this to protect her. You tell her and she'll want to get involved. Even though she's good, it don't make sense for her to go pickin' a fight with Rixon and his men. It's better she stays just bein' around to protect us and the prospectors.'

Shane nodded.

'OK,' he said. 'I w-won't s-say nothin' to her.' He got up. 'I'll s-see you all l-later.'

'Don't leave it too late,' said Billy Joe. 'We wanna start listenin' soon as it gets dark. If you ain't back, I'm goin' anyway.'

'I-I'll be b-back,' Shane assured him. Then he set off for his mother's tent.

CHAPTER 14

Shane sat outside the tent with his mother and sister. Em had been washed now after her day spent digging, and was sitting playing with her rag doll, cuddling it and talking to it. Kitty Kelly was smiling.

'You happy, M-Ma?' Shane asked.

'I got my son back,' she told Shane. 'That's somethin' I thought would never happen again.' She looked at Shane. 'Ain't you happy at that?'

Shane nodded, then said seriously, 'I'd be ha-happier if you wasn't a g-gunfighter.'

Kelly laughed.

'We all do what we're good at, Shane,' she said. 'I didn't choose gunfightin', it sort of chose me, like I told you.'

'But you could get killed!' said Shane. He gestured at his little sister, playing happily. 'What happens to Em if you get killed?'

Kitty Kelly looked at Shane and sighed.

'People die whatever they do,' she said. 'Cattlemen die from cows tramplin' them. I seen a man fall off a boardwalk and bang his head on a post and die. People who never carry a gun catch a disease and die. There ain't no way you can stop yourself from dyin', Shane.'

'Yes, b-but you're more likely to d-die if y-you're a g-gunfighter.'

'Not if you're a good one,' said Kelly. 'Word gets out you're good, people don't trouble you. Like today. No one got killed, just one gunman got wounded. That's it.'

Shane shook his head, unconvinced.

'Th-that ain't the w-way it is, Ma,' he said. 'I s-seen it. S-someone g-gets a rep-reputation for b-bein' g-good with a g-gun, people wanna try 'em out.' He dropped his eyes. 'An I ain't j-just th-thinkin' of Em. I th-thought you w-was dead. N-now you ain't an' I f-found you again. I d-don't want you d-dyin' on me and losin' you now. I saw P-Pete shot d-dead, s-savin' my life. It n-near k-killed me!'

Kitty Kelly leaned forward and rested her hand gently on her son's shoulder.

'You won't lose me, Shane,' she said. 'As long as I'm alive, you won't lose me again.'

'But ain't th-that the thing, Ma! As l-long as you're alive! You're a g-gunfighter!'

'Trust me, Shane. I'm staying alive.'

* ✸ *

Dusk was falling as Shane returned to the gang, the sky turning from a reddish gold to deep dark blue. Billy Joe was ready to go.

'I wondered if you was comin',' he said.

'That's w-why I'm here,' Shane told him firmly.

The two boys set off through the township of tents. Most of the prospectors were sitting outside by their fires, cooking their suppers and brewing coffee in blackened pots. Some had already gone to bed, their tent flaps closed, ready for an early start the next day.

Billy Joe and Shane left the tents and made for Farley's wagons, which stood apart from everyone else. Next to the two store wagons were three tents, where Rixon and his gunmen slept. There was no sign of any fires burning.

'I guess they must all be inside the store wagons,' muttered Billy Joe.

The two boys crept forward, keeping watch the whole time in case anyone suddenly appeared. They made it to the wagons, and crept along their length to the middle where the two vehicles joined, at a point where they knew Farley's private room and his office were. They could hear angry voices coming from inside. Although the wagons were made of wood, it was mostly so thin it wasn't much thicker than several layers of cloth. Farley's voice was the loudest.

'You let that woman show you up!' he raged. 'Six of you and you let one woman make you back off!'

'She just got lucky!' Rixon snapped back.

'That ain't the way I heard it!' shouted Farley. 'The way I heard it she beat you to the draw.'

'Only cos I wasn't expectin' it,' retorted Rixon. 'Next time she won't be so lucky. I'm planning on calling her out tomorrow in front of everyone. Then me and the boys will just shoot her down.'

'You fool,' snapped Farley. 'You think she's gonna let that happen? This woman ain't just good with a gun, she's got *brains*! She outsmarted you, and everyone saw! You know what that means?'

'It means she's dead,' growled Rixon.

'No, it means that people here are startin' to question whether you're worth the money they're payin' me. *I'm* startin' to question whether you and this bunch of clowns are worth the money!'

'She just got lucky, Mr Farley!' protested a new voice, Dan.

'And she won't be so lucky tomorrow,' added Rixon menacingly.

'Yeah, but say she is,' insisted Farley. 'If she faces you down tomorrow, it's all over. And what do I get out of it? Nothin'! No one's gonna pay me a red cent if she beats you.'

'There's six of us!' protested Dan. 'What can she do against six of us?'

'There's five of you without Scrub,' Farley snapped back. 'And she can do the same tomorrow as she did today. No, we gotta come up with somethin' better. Somethin' clever. Somethin' that makes her clear out and not come back!'

Suddenly Billy Joe heard Rixon chuckle.

'I got an idea!' he said, and the way he said it sent a chill through Billy Joe. There was real nastiness in his voice, a delight in doing something evil.

Then Rixon's voice dropped to a whisper. Billy Joe pressed against the side of the wagon, straining to hear, but he couldn't make out the words. Because he was concentrating so hard on trying to hear what the gunman was saying, he didn't hear the footsteps coming up behind him. The first sound he was aware of was an angry shout of, 'Hey, you!'

It sparked Billy Joe into immediate action. Spurred on by his instinct for self survival, he ran as fast as he could, not even looking back to see who had appeared.

He threw a frantic shout of, 'Run, Shane!' over his shoulder and didn't stop until he reached the cover of a patch of undergrowth and bushes. He threw himself into the bushes and then turned, expecting to see his friend close behind him. Instead, he was shocked to see that Shane was struggling in the one-handed grip of Scrub, the gunman with the broken arm.

The door of the store wagon burst open and Rixon and Farley came crashing out. Rixon leapt down the steps, grabbed hold of the struggling Shane and struck him hard across the face.

'Keep still, boy!' he roared. 'Or next time it'll be a bullet you receive!'

Shane stopped struggling and let himself be held.

'I was just comin' from the tent and I saw him and this other kid,' said Scrub. 'They was listenin' outside the wagon.'

Rixon and the others looked around.

'What happened to his friend?' demanded Farley.

'I don't know,' said Scrub. 'He just disappeared.'

Farley pointed at the store wagon.

'Take the boy inside,' he ordered.

'Why?' asked one of the gunmen.

'Because I want to know just how much he heard,' said Farley.

'Say he don't talk?' asked one of the gunmen.

'He'll talk,' growled Rixon.

With that, Rixon nodded and dragged Shane up the steps and inside the wagon. Then the other men followed, and the door slammed shut.

Damn! thought Billy Joe.

CHAPTER 15

Billy Joe crouched behind the cover of the bushes, his eyes fixed firmly on the store wagon. He was cold and tired. He'd been here for he didn't know how long. It felt like hours. He wanted to get back to the tent and tell Jess what had happened, but he didn't dare move. Farley's men had Shane. He had to know what was going to happen to his friend.

* * *

Inside the wagon, Shane sat on the hard wooden chair, doing his best not to show how scared he was. But he *was* scared. The six men who stood menacingly around him all had grim determined expressions on their faces. Shane wasn't sure who was the most frightening: Farley, with his greedy look that showed he'd do anything for money, or Rixon, who stared at Shane with an insane, unstable look in his eyes. The two men were different in the way they went about things as well – Farley had that dreadful fake smile on his face and tried to appear calm, while Rixon jerked and stomped about like he was ready to explode into action at any second.

'What did you hear, boy?' asked Farley, still smiling with his mouth, while his piggy eyes bored deep into Shane's. 'It'd be a good idea for you to tell us.'

Shane remained silent. He just swallowed and returned Farley's stare.

'Ain't no use talkin' nice to him!' Rixon burst out suddenly. 'Threaten him! Tell him you'll cut off one of his fingers if he don't talk!' Suddenly he pulled out a knife. 'I'll do it myself if you won't!'

'Easy, Duke,' said Farley soothingly. 'We don't need that kind of violence.'

Rixon pushed Farley aside and thrust his angry face just a few inches from Shane's.

'What were you doin' outside the wagon?' he demanded.

'N-n-n-' stammered Shane.

One of the other men laughed.

'Yeah, I remember now!' he chuckled. 'This here's the kid with the stammer! You ain't gonna get him to talk. Not so's you can understand what he's sayin', anyhow!'

'Shut up!' snarled Rixon.

Then Farley turned on Rixon. His smile had gone for the moment.

'No, *you* shut up, Duke,' he said quietly. 'And put that knife away.' He turned back to Shane. 'This boy will talk in good time.'

Rixon scowled, but put the knife away. 'Time is the thing we ain't got,' he snapped. 'We need to put the plan into operation now and get rid of this Kitty Kelly, before we lose what we got here altogether.'

Farley studied Shane, then nodded.

'I think you may be right, Duke,' he agreed. 'But we do it without any noise. Nice and quiet.'

Shane's mind was in a whirl. *What was their plan?* He had to find out, and he had to get that information to the rest of the gang, and his ma.

* * *

As Billy Joe crouched and stared at the wagons, he heard footsteps approaching, and he whirled round, ready to run again. But it was Jess.

'Billy Joe, where in tarnation you been?' demanded Jess angrily. 'I expected you and Shane back long before this! I had to leave Andy on his own and come and find you.' He looked around. 'Where *is* Shane?'

Billy Joe gestured towards the store wagons.

'He's in there,' he said. 'Farley and Rixon caught him.'

For a moment Jess was stunned into silence. He jerked round and looked towards the wagons, letting the thought of Shane's capture sink in.

'You sure they ain't killed him?'

Billy Joe shook his head.

'I'm pretty sure Shane's still alive,' he said. 'I heard Farley say they needed to find out what he might've heard, just before they took him in. We gotta get him out of there.'

'Any ideas on how to do that?' asked Jess.

'Not really,' admitted Billy Joe. 'I bin sittin' here lookin' at them wagons, and they look pretty sturdy to me. There's six of them in there with Shane, countin' Farley. The one Kitty Kelly shot, Scrub, is in one of them tents. My thought was for you an' me to take turns in watchin' till they bring Shane out, and then for us to try somethin'.'

Jess looked towards the store wagons standing there in the twilight. Suddenly they heard noises coming from their direction as the door opened, and both boys ducked down. As they watched they saw three men come down the steps and head towards the tents. Billy Joe recognised who they were.

'By my reckonin' there's now just Farley, Rixon and Dan left in the store wagons with Shane,' he mused.

'I still don't like those odds,' muttered Jess.

'You reckon one of us ought to go fetch Kitty Kelly?' suggested Billy Joe.

'I don't know,' murmured Jess doubtfully. 'If she hears about Shane bein' taken, she's likely gonna come in with all guns blazin'. There's gunpowder an' stuff in that store. It only needs one bullet to hit it and the whole store goes up.'

'We can't *not* tell her,' insisted Billy Joe. 'She sure as hell is gonna notice if Shane ain't around.'

Jess sighed heavily.

'You're right,' he said. He looked towards the wagons. 'You OK keeping watch for a while longer, Billy Joe?' he asked.

'Sure,' nodded Billy Joe. 'You gonna go tell Shane's ma?'

'Guess I'm gonna have to,' sighed Jess.

❋ ❋ ❋

'Miz Kelly!'

Jess stood outside Kitty Kelly's tent in the darkness and gave a whispered call, loud enough so that he hoped she heard, but not loud enough to disturb anyone else. There was no immediate response. *Maybe she's fast asleep*, he thought. *Even gunfighters have to sleep some time*. He cleared his throat and opened his mouth to call again, just a bit louder this time, 'Miz –'

'Ssh!' Kitty Kelly had appeared in the opening of the tent, gun in hand. 'You'll wake Em.' She peered left and right, still holding the gun, obviously alerted to the fact that something was wrong by the tone of Jess's voice.

'It's OK, you can put the gun away,' Jess assured her.

Kelly hesitated, took one last look around to make sure they were safe, then slid the gun back into its holster. She was fully dressed. At least, she was wearing jeans and a shirt. *She must sleep with her gun*, thought Jess. *And sleep darned light too*. He guessed that was the life of a gunfighter – always expecting someone to come after you.

'What's the matter?' she asked. 'What's wrong?'

'Farley and Rixon have got Shane,' said Jess.

'What?! Where?'

'In the store wagon.'

Kelly pushed her way out of the tent, bringing her gunbelt with her, and she began to buckle it on. In the twilight Jess could see the tight expression on her face.

'You can't go after them!' he said. 'There's six men there, all armed.'

'They've got my son!' she snapped. She sat down on the ground, reached into the tent and pulled out her boots, then began pulling them on. 'You stay here and watch Em for me,' she told him.

'No!' insisted Jess. 'That's not why I came. I'm here to work out how we can rescue Shane without him or you gettin' hurt. You go bustin' in there, Shane's as likely to get shot as anyone. At the moment he's safe and alive.'

Kelly studied Jess.

'How d'you know?' she asked.

As quickly as he could, Jess told her what had happened – how the boys were sure that Farley and Rixon were up to something bad. How Billy Joe and Shane had gone off to eavesdrop on them at the store wagons. And how Shane had been captured, but Billy Joe had got away and was now keeping watch on the store wagons.

'The problem is they got gunpowder and explosives and all sorts of ammunition inside the wagon. If you go in and there's a gunfight, a bullet could set it all off and Shane will die for sure.'

Kelly thought about it, then nodded.

'That's good thinking, Jess,' she said. 'OK, so we keep watch on the store wagons. They're gonna have to take Shane outside sooner or later. Seems to me it'll be safer to try and free him out in the open than inside with that gunpowder an' stuff sittin' there.'

'That's what we was thinking,' agreed Jess.

'OK,' nodded Kelly. 'We'll go and join Billy Joe, stake out the wagons, see what I can come up with. But who's gonna watch over Em?'

Jess gestured towards a large tent a short distance away.

'How about the Bartletts?' he suggested. 'I'm pretty sure Jane or Betty would watch her, if you asked.'

Kelly weighed up Jess's suggestion, then nodded.

'OK,' she agreed. 'Stay here while I go and speak to them. Then we'll go and do what needs doin'.'

CHAPTER 16

Shane sat on the chair under Dan's watchful eye. Farley and Rixon stood apart, whispering together.

They're planning something, thought Shane. He looked at Dan, and then towards the door of the wagon. *While Farley and Rixon were engrossed in their conversation, maybe he could make a break for it. Leap at Dan, kick him, and be out through the door before the two others could make a move.* At least, he hoped so. He knew Rixon was fast with a gun. But that wasn't what held him back from trying. He needed to find out what their plan was for his ma.

Suddenly Farley moved away from Rixon and joined Shane and Dan.

'OK, Dan,' he said. 'You know what you've got to do. But do it quiet.'

Dan nodded, and then left. Rixon walked over to the wagon door and locked it behind him.

'Just in case you're thinking of makin' a break for it,' he sneered at Shane.

'I ain't sc-scared of you!' said Shane defiantly. 'That l-lady gunfighter sh-showed you up good!'

Rixon's face contorted with fury.

'Yeah! Well she ain't gonna show anyone up soon!' he stormed. 'Not once we –'

'Rixon!' snapped Farley. He held up a warning finger. 'Let's not give away our secrets, eh!' He gestured at the walls of wagon. 'You never know who might be listenin'.'

Rixon scowled, then turned away. Farley gave Shane his cold smile.

'Unless you already know what we've got in mind for her,' he said. 'What *did* you hear?'

* * *

Billy Joe felt like he'd been watching the store wagons for so long that they were starting to change shape before his eyes. There had been no movement at all, except once. The door had opened, making Billy Joe strain his eyes even more, ready to take action if Shane appeared. But it had just been one of the gunmen, Dan, who'd come out and then gone off into the night. Since then, nothing.

He heard footsteps approaching and turned to see Jess and Kitty Kelly arrive.

'What's happening?' asked Jess.

'Everything's still the same as before, 'cept Dan went out from the wagon a short while ago. Maybe he's gone to the toilet.' Billy Joe frowned thoughtfully. 'Though he's takin' a long time over it.'

Kitty Kelly crouched in the cover of the bushes, studying the wagons.

'That where they got Shane?' she asked.

'That's where they took him,' Billy Joe nodded.

Kitty Kelly continued studying the wagons.

'Which is the one with the gunpowder and ammunition and stuff?' she asked.

Briefly, Jess and Billy Joe filled her in. They added what they knew about the living arrangements – Farley slept in the store wagon while Rixon and his men were in the three tents, two to a tent.

Kelly looked up at the sky.

'It's gonna be daylight in a couple of hours,' she said. 'I'm gonna go back to my tent and come up with somethin' to bust Shane out of there. You boys OK for keepin' watch a while longer?'

'No problem,' nodded Jess. 'I'll stay here.' He turned to Billy Joe. 'You'd better get back to our tent. Andy's bin left on his own a long while now. You know what he's like for getting into scrapes when he's on his own. There's no knowin' what him and that fool dog might have got up to.'

'They should both be asleep,' murmured Billy Joe.

'They *should*,' agreed Jess.

'Come on, Billy Joe,' muttered Kelly. 'We'll get back to the tents and I'll figure out a way to deal with this.'

With that, she stood up and moved silently off.

'I'll be back just before daylight,' Billy Joe promised Jess, then he followed after Kelly.

Jess remained crouched behind the bushes, his attention fully on the wagons and the three tents. The problem was the gunpowder. He was sure that Kelly could handle herself if it came to a gunfight, but that gunpowder sitting in the store made it dangerous. They had to get Shane out of there without guns being fired!

Suddenly he heard footsteps in the distance, moving fast. He ducked down and peered through the bushes. A man was hurrying towards the wagons. It looked like he'd come from the direction of the township of tents, and he was carrying something that looked like a sack. The man reached the steps of the wagons and grunted, 'It's me!'

It was Dan.

The door was unlocked and Jess saw Rixon framed in the doorway by the light of the oil lamp. Dan climbed up the stairs, and as he did so the sack in his arms moved, and Jess realised it wasn't a sack, it was a child in a dress.

It was Em!

CHAPTER 17

Shane stood up, shocked, as he saw his little sister carried into the wagon and dumped on the ground.

'Em!'

Em got up from the floor and ran to her brother and threw her arms around him.

'Now ain't that touching!' sneered Rixon.

Em turned on the gunman.

'You leave my brother and me alone!' she snapped.

Rixon, Dan and Farley exchanged surprised looks.

'Well, well, so you're Kitty Kelly's kid too,' chuckled Rixon. 'Wonder how many others she's got hanging around.'

'D-don't you s-say b-bad things about m-my ma!' stormed Shane.

Rixon laughed.

'W-why n-not?' he mimicked.

Farley nodded thoughtfully.

'This is even better than we hoped,' he said. 'We got *both* her kids. Now that's what I call *real* bargaining power!' He smiled at the gunmen. 'I don't think we'll have any problems persuading Miz Kelly to leave now, fellas!'

* * *

We got your kid. Quit this place if you want her to live.

Kitty Kelly held the scrap of paper in her hand and read it again. Billy Joe saw the anger on her face, which was terrifying to see. He'd just poked his head into his own tent and seen that Andy and Patch were still fast asleep when he'd heard the howl of rage from Kitty Kelly. He'd hurried over to her tent and found the gunfighter with the four members of the Bartlett family and the scrawled note.

Jane Bartlett sobbed, 'The man held a gun at me! I didn't know what else to do!'

Kelly didn't say a word. She screwed up the piece of paper and then turned and headed back the way she'd come.

'It wasn't Jane's fault,' Ed Bartlett appealed to Billy Joe. 'She was facing a gun! I didn't know anything about it until afterwards, or I'd have done something.'

'I know that, Mr Bartlett,' nodded Billy Joe. He looked at the four stunned members of the Bartlett family. 'I'd better go after Miz Kelly,' he told them. 'There's gonna be trouble.'

'You're right,' Ed Bartlett nodded grimly. Turning to his son he said, 'Chris, get my gunbelt and holster from the tent.'

Jane Bartlett rushed to her husband and threw her arms around him.

'Ed, you can't! Those men are killers! They'll shoot you down!'

Ed Bartlett gently removed his wife's arms from around him.

'Jane, those men took a little baby girl and they're threatenin' to kill her. What sort of parents are we if we let that happen?'

'You're good parents, Mr Bartlett,' said Billy Joe. 'And don't let anyone tell you different. But this ain't your fight.'

'Yes, it is,' said Ed Bartlett. 'And it shoulda bin my fight before this, then it wouldn't have got this far.' Turning again to his son, who still stood, hesitating, unsure what to do, he said, 'Chris, didn't you hear what I said? Go get my gunbelt and holster for me.'

✴ ✴ ✴

Billy Joe hurried back to where he'd left Jess watching the store wagons. Kitty Kelly was already there and she whirled round as she heard him arrive, her gun held ready. She lowered it when she saw it was Billy Joe.

'Ed Bartlett's comin' behind me,' Billy Joe told them. 'He's bringin' a gun.'

'He's a good man,' she Kelly. She frowned, her face troubled. 'But I don't want him gettin' hurt. These people hired me to protect 'em, not the other way round.'

'I reckon they feel we're all in this together,' said Jess quietly.

Kelly took this in, then nodded.

'I never say no to good help,' she said. 'OK, Jess, where exactly are these varmints?'

'Dan took Em into the store wagon,' Jess told her. 'Shane, Farley and Rixon are in there as well.'

'And the others?'

'Still in their tents, like before.' He gestured at the tents. 'Scrub's in that far one on his own, but he's got that busted arm. Adam and Jeb are in that first tent; Tag's in the second one. There ain't been no movement from any of 'em, so I guess they're asleep.'

'OK,' nodded Kelly. 'It's time to level the odds. But let's see if we can do this without shootin'. Any gunfire is gonna let Farley know I'm here. The longer we can keep him from knowin' that, the better.' She looked at Billy Joe. 'Reckon you can help me, Billy Joe?'

'Sure can,' nodded Billy Joe.

To Jess she said, 'When Ed Bartlett arrives, tell him to wait here with you.'

Jess nodded. Kitty Kelly looked towards the tents.

'OK, Billy Joe,' she said. 'Let's go deal with some bad guys.'

CHAPTER 18

Billy Joe hurried after Kitty Kelly. He'd sounded confident when he'd told the gunfighter he could help her, now it had come to it his throat felt dry and his heart was pounding so much he felt sure that anyone near him would be able to hear it thumping. He was going up against armed gunmen, and without a weapon!

Kelly crouched low as she moved. She got to the first tent and listened. They could hear the sounds of two men snoring. Kelly looked at Billy Joe, then put her finger to her lips.

'Stay here and keep an eye on the tent where Tag is, and the store wagons,' she whispered. 'Anyone comes, you call!'

Billy Joe nodded, and took up his position by the tent flap. Kelly slipped into the tent. Billy Joe strained to listen. He heard the two men snoring, then a sudden *thump*! as a gun was used as a club. He heard a muttered and dazed 'what?' and then the sound of that *thump*! again.

A few seconds later, Kitty Kelly poked her head back through the tent flap.

'You any good at tyin' knots?' she asked.

Billy Joe nodded. Andy was forever practising tying new knots and he'd shown Billy Joe a few good ones.

'Then get in here and tie these two up,' said Kitty Kelly. 'They shouldn't give you any trouble.'

Billy Joe let her come out of the tent, then he slipped inside. Adam and Jeb lay on the ground, unconscious. Billy Joe spotted some coils of thin rope on one side of the tent. He took a coil and began to tie the rope around Jeb's ankles, and then ran it up to Jeb's wrists and tied them together, pulling it tight so that the man's feet were pulled up behind him. There was no way that Jeb could stand up now.

That done, Billy Joe turned to Adam and did the same to him. Then he took the kerchief from around the neck of each man, forced it into their mouths, and tied the end tight behind their heads to keep them silent. All the time, both men stayed out cold.

Billy Joe left the tent, and found Kelly emerging from Tag's tent.

'That's him trussed up like a chicken,' she whispered.

Billy Joe gestured toward the other tent.

'What about Scrub?' he asked.

'I left him till last,' she murmured. She gave a cold grin. 'Ain't nothin' he can do with that busted arm.'

She turned towards the third tent, and as she did so the tent flap parted and Scrub looked out. His mouth fell open in surprise as he saw Kelly and Billy Joe.

'What the –' he began. Then he yelled, 'Duke! Help!'

Smack!

Kitty Kelly leapt forward and smashed her pistol into Scrub's face and he crumpled to the ground. Then she turned towards the store wagon. But before she could turn properly, the door burst open and Rixon stood there, gun in hand.

Bang!

Both guns fired at once; Kelly's bullet smashing into the wood of the store wagon door, tearing through it. Immediately Rixon slammed the door shut.

Then, as Billy watched, Kelly collapsed to the ground.

Shane leapt to his feet.

'What's going on?' he demanded.

'Guess your ma ain't taking our offer,' snarled Rixon. Then he smiled. 'But I think I hit her.'

'You *think*?' shouted Farley, his smile disappearing for once.

Rixon gestured towards the door. 'I saw her go down, and there ain't been no more shooting since.'

Suddenly Em ran forward and began to beat at him with her tiny fists, her face screwed up in tears.

'You kill my ma!' she hollered. 'You kill my ma!'

Roughly, Rixon grabbed Em and threw her towards Shane.

'You take care of this,' he snarled. 'Else I will.'

Shane looked white-faced as he gathered his crying sister in his arms.

'It'll be OK, Em,' he said gently, trying to calm her down. 'I'm sure Ma's OK.'

But was she? Had his ma been shot dead by Rixon? Or was she outside even now, making plans to rescue them?

Farley's calm composure had deserted him. He paced around the room.

'We have to find out if she's dead,' he muttered. 'If she ain't, we got ourselves a whole heap of trouble.'

'Not while we've got these two,' said Rixon, gesturing at Shane and Em.

'Hey, Rixon!'

The call from outside came from Kitty Kelly, there was no doubt about that. Shane and Em's faces lit up with delight as they heard their mother's voice calling out clear as a bell.

Farley's face twisted with fury and he turned on Rixon.

'You fool! You said you'd shot her! Does that sound like a woman who's been shot?'

The confident smirk had been wiped off Rixon's face, and he gaped at Farley and Dan.

'I did!' he insisted. 'I saw her go down!'

'Rixon!' came Kelly's voice again.

Rixon hesitated, then he shouted back through the closed door, 'What?'

'I got a proposition for you!' called Kelly. 'You let my kids go, and I let you and your men ride outta here.'

Rixon hesitated. Shane could see the anger and indecision on his face. Then he decided to bluff it out. He forced a harsh laugh.

'You ain't got nothin', lady gunfighter!' he shouted. 'I shot you! I saw you go down! I know you're hurt real bad!'

There was a pause, then Kelly shouted back, 'My pride's hurt, that's all! Yeah, you winged me, but it ain't nothin' but a flesh wound. It may stop me sittin' down fer a day or two, but it don't stop me usin' these here guns!'

With that, she let fly a shot that tore a hole in the top of the wooden door.

'We're sunk!' groaned Farley. 'She's got us!'

'No lady gunfighter gets the better of me,' snarled Rixon. He hesitated again, and then shouted, 'What's happened to Jeb and the others? Have you killed my men?'

'No, they're still alive, Rixon!' came Kelly's shouted response. 'Trussed up like chickens, so they ain't gonna be no use to you. I ain't got no quarrel with them, providin' they back off. Same as for you. Just let my kids go and we can all walk away from this!'

'That might be best, Duke,' said Dan, speaking for the first time. 'There ain't no other way out of this wagon. If we go out through that door guns blazin', she'll kill us for sure.'

Farley stared at Dan, furious.

'Am I hearing right?' he demanded, his voice almost a shriek. 'I've paid you good money, and now you're prepared to run away! From a woman!'

'This ain't no ordinary woman, Mr Farley,' said Dan. 'We're trapped here.' He turned to Rixon, his voice whining as he appealed. 'What d'you say, Duke?'

Rixon nodded thoughtfully.

'It might be the only way out of here in the short term,' he said. Then his face hardened. 'But I sure ain't letting her run off so easy. Once we leave here, we're coming back and finishing her and all these other stinkin' prospectors!'

Farley rushed over to Rixon and grabbed him by the front of his shirt.

'You're leaving?' he demanded, anger in his voice.

'Just for the moment,' nodded Rixon. 'Then we'll come back and settle with her when we're ready.'

'Oh no, you don't!' raged Farley. 'I won't let you

leave me here unprotected against that woman! She'll kill me!'

'Maybe she will and maybe she won't,' nodded Rixon.

Farley stood glaring at Rixon, shaking. Then he let go of the gunman's shirt and stormed to the door.

'No deal, lady!' he shouted through the closed door. 'You know how much money I've got invested in this place? You leave, and then you get your kids back when I'm ready.'

'Guess you ain't thinkin' properly, Farley!' Kelly called back. 'If this here turns into a shootin' match, you got a whole load of gunpowder in that wagon that'll blow you all to kingdom come!'

'She's right, boss,' murmured Dan.

'No, she ain't,' said Farley vehemently. Through the door, he shouted, 'That ain't gonna happen, Kelly! You wouldn't risk your kids!'

'You're gonna kill 'em anyway,' shouted Kelly. 'Least this way, I know you're dead as well.'

'You're bluffing!' shouted Farley.

'You know I ain't bluffin'!' Kelly shouted back. 'That bullet hole I put in your door right above your heads ought to convince you of that.'

Rixon stepped forward and thrust Farley to one side, then called out, 'I want some kind of guarantee me and my men won't be harmed!'

Shane held Em tighter, a feeling of elation filling

him. His ma had done it. She'd saved them. The gunmen were going to let them go!

'I give you my word!' called Kelly.

As Shane watched, Rixon shook his head.

'That ain't good enough!' he shouted back. 'I want safe passage with no one following. When we're far enough away, I'll let the kids go.'

No, thought Shane. *It's a trick. Don't trust him, Ma*!

Farley was beside himself with anger as he heard Rixon's words.

'Oh no, you don't!' he yelled, throwing himself at Rixon. 'You ain't leavin' me on my own! All my money's tied up here!'

In answer, Rixon drew back his fist and punched Farley in the face. The store owner stumbled back and fell to the floor. Rixon levelled his gun at Farley.

'You ain't in charge of us no more, Farley,' he said.

✹ ✹ ✹

Outside, Billy Joe, Jess and Ed Bartlett watched Kitty Kelly, and Billy Joe marvelled at the woman's strength. During the whole exchange with Rixon she'd sounded like a woman in control, a woman fit to carry on the fight. But the truth was Rixon's bullet had done real damage to her, tearing her up somewhere inside.

She lay there, propped up against a huge rock, her already pale face even whiter, sweat pouring down it.

Her pistol hung limply from her hand. She looked like she was dying.

'You can't do much against 'em, the state you're in,' warned Jess.

'I can so long as Rixon don't know how bad he shot me,' said Kelly. She breathed hard, biting her lip again, then she called out, 'What's it to be, Rixon?'

The door of the wagon sprang open. Farley was pushed out and came tumbling down the steps.

Kelly lifted her pistol, then lowered it again as she saw the tiny figure of Em standing in the doorway in front of Rixon. He held onto her with one hand, while his man, Dan, held a pistol pointed at Em's head.

'Take a shot and one of us shoots this kid,' Rixon warned.

'Let her go!' called Kelly.

'Nope,' said Rixon flatly.

Sam Farley pulled himself to his feet. He dusted the dirt off his clothes and glared at Rixon.

'You can't do a deal without me!' he shouted. 'These are my wagons! It's my money! This is all mine!'

In answer, Rixon pointed his gun at Farley and pulled the trigger twice. The first shot caught Farley in the centre of the chest and sent him staggering backwards. The second brought him crashing to the ground, where he lay dead, his eyes wide open, a look of surprise on his face, blood trickling out from his chest.

'Now it's just between you and me, Kelly!' called Rixon. 'Let me and my men take a run for it with this wagon, and you get your kids back. Either that or we all die. And these kids'll be the first.'

With that, Rixon slammed the door shut.

CHAPTER 19

Inside the store wagon, Rixon pushed Em towards Shane. Em stumbled, but Shane caught her and stopped her from falling.

'Here, kid,' snapped Rixon. 'Look after her. Make sure you both stay quiet. Try anything and you get what Farley got.' Then he turned to Dan. 'Dan, lock that door and keep that key somewhere safe. We don't want anyone bustin' in an' surprisin' us, or these two makin' a run for it. Right now, they're our only ticket out of here.'

'Think she'll let us go?' asked Dan.

Rixon gave a smug smile.

'We got her kids. Course she'll let us go. Especially after she saw me shoot Farley. She knows I mean business.'

With that, Rixon walked to where the hardware had been stacked inside the store wagon. He took boxes of bullets down from the shelves, opened one and began reloading his pistols.

'Better get ourselves ready in case there's more gunplay,' he muttered.

Dan locked the door and then joined Rixon reloading his guns.

Em began to sniffle, wiping her nose against the tears. Shane saw that she was shaking. He sat down beside his little sister and put his arms around her, cuddling her to him.

'I'm scared,' she whispered.

'It's g-gonna be O-OK, Em,' he said softly. 'Ma and J-Jess an' B-Billy Joe will g-get us out of this, s-see if they d-don't.'

* * *

Kitty Kelly lay face down on the ground, clenching her teeth against the pain as Ed Bartlett gently prodded around the wound in her back. Her shirt had been pulled up and they could see the entry wound where the bullet had gone in.

'There ain't no exit wound,' muttered Bartlett. 'Means the bullet's still in there somewhere.' He pulled down her shirt. 'You're gonna need a doc to take it out.'

Kelly forced herself up and then turned so she was in a sitting position.

'I ain't got time for no doc,' she said.

There was a clatter of boots, and then Jimmy Flynn and Robert Jackson appeared, both carrying rifles.

'We heard what happened, Rixon takin' your daughter,' said Jimmy Flynn. He shook his head apologetically. 'I should never have got you into this, Miz Kelly.'

'I come into it of my own free will,' muttered Kelly. 'So I'm gonna finish it.'

'You ain't in no fit state,' said Ed Bartlett. He turned to Flynn and Robert and explained, 'Rixon shot her. The bullet's inside her somewhere low down. I'm guessin' it ain't far from her stomach.' He turned back to Kelly and said severely, 'If you don't lie still that bullet could move around inside and kill you.'

'I ain't lyin' still while that scum's got my kids,' retorted Kelly. 'Bandage me up as best you can an' stop the bleedin'.'

Ed Bartlett hesitated, then nodded. He took a roll of linen from a bag slung round his shoulder and began to tear it into strips.

'What d'you want us to do?' asked Flynn.

'Just keep an eye on that wagon,' said Kelly, wincing as Ed Bartlett set to work on her.

'What you plannin'?' asked Robert.

'I'm still thinkin',' muttered Kelly.

'Maybe we could shoot 'em out?' suggested Robert.

'And risk killin' them two kids?' Flynn pointed out.

'And there's gunpowder in there,' Billy Joe added. 'A gunfight would set it off.'

'I got an idea,' said Jess. He pointed to the top of the store wagon, where bales of cloth and wooden crates and other stores had been lashed to the roof. 'If me and Billy Joe get up there and hide ourselves among all that stuff, you can let 'em leave. But Billy Joe and me'll be goin' with 'em.'

Billy Joe looked at Jess, stunned.

'That is the most foolish and dangerous idea I ever heard in my life!' Then he smiled. 'And the cleverest!'

'It sure is a real good idea,' murmured Kelly. 'If I can get me up on that roof as well we might be able to do somethin'.'

Billy Joe looked at her with an expression of amazement.

'Beggin' your pardon, Miz Kelly, but you can hardly move and you're like to die if you do, cos of that bullet inside you!' he said.

Kitty Kelly looked Billy Joe firmly in the face.

'If I had ten bullets in me it wouldn't stop me tryin' to get my kids out of this,' she said. 'Just get me on that roof with my guns and I'll do the rest.' Then she propped herself up and shouted towards the store wagon, 'OK, Rixon! You got your deal. You can go, but we hang onto your men until the kids are free.'

There was a pause, then Rixon shouted back through the door.

'No deal!' he said. 'My men or nothin'!'

'Then it'd better be nothin'!' Kelly replied. 'We'd be foolish not to have some kinda guarantee you'll let those kids go. As soon as we get them back, your men go free.'

There was a pause, then Rixon demanded, 'How do I know you won't kill 'em?'

'Same way I know you won't kill those kids!' Kelly shouted back.

There was another pause, then Rixon yelled, 'OK. But I'm gonna need one of my men to help Dan hitch up the team of horses!'

'Then there'll be *three* gunmen!' mutterred Billy Joe, not liking the odds.

'We ain't got no choice, Billy Joe,' said Jess. 'We gotta let 'em start that wagon rollin', then we make our move.' He turned to Flynn, Robert and Bartlett. 'If you tie up Scrub and then untie one of the other gunment, that should give us time to get on that there roof.'

Flynn nodded.

'Leave it to us,' he said.

'You're gonna have to make sure the one you untie don't see us,' warned Billy Joe.

Flynn gave Billy Joe a hard look.

'Son, I bin around since long before you was born. You don't need to tell me things someone with half a brain could work out for himself.'

Billy Joe bowed his head.

'Sorry, Mr Flynn,' he said. 'Guess I'm just worried about us gettin' up on that roof, and then stayin' up there alive.'

Flynn nodded.

'Understood, son. Don't worry, we won't let them varmints see what you're doin'.' He turned to Kelly. 'You still think you can get yourself up on that roof?'

Kelly gritted her teeth and nodded.

'I'll do it or die tryin',' she said.

'OK,' said Flynn. 'Me and Robert here will do the tyin' up. Ed, you keep us all covered, case they try anythin' sneaky.'

'Got it,' nodded Bartlett. He held his rifle aimed towards the store wagon.

'Time to start the action,' murmured Kelly. She pushed herself up into a sitting position and shouted, 'OK, Rixon! In a few minutes the boys are gonna untie one of your men so he can help you with the horses. If I see any sign of that door openin' while they're doin' it, I'll shoot your men dead. Is that clear?'

There was a pause, then Rixon shouted back, 'Clear!'

Kelly pushed herself up until she was in a crouching position. She was obviously in pain. She turned to Jess and Billy Joe.

'You boys OK for this?' she asked.

'They got our friend,' Jess assured her. 'We're gonna get him and Em outta there.'

'OK,' she said. 'Let's go.'

CHAPTER 20

The sun was getting higher in the sky. The early cold of dawn had been replaced by a harsher heat.

Jess, Billy Joe and Kitty Kelly watched as Jimmy Flynn and Robert went towards the tents near the store wagon. Once they were there, and were sure they'd hauled the injured Scrub out of sight, they set off from their hiding place towards the back of the store wagon. They moved at a crouch, Kitty Kelly stumbling and dragging as she moved. Jess was worried in case Rixon had found a hole in the wooden boards to look through, but they were in luck. They made it to the wagon with no shots coming from inside.

Once there, they crept to the ladder by the back door that ran up to the roof. It was obvious to Billy Joe from the pain etched on Kelly's face that every step had been agony, but the gunfighter was determined to do it. She crumpled to her knees beside the ladder, head bowed, recovering her strength. Jess and Billy Joe watched on with concern, but she looked up and shook her head, then put a finger to her lips to make sure they stayed silent.

Kelly gritted her teeth, then forced herself to her feet, reached up and grabbed hold of the ladder. She lifted a boot, put it on the first rung, and then hauled herself up. Billy Joe could tell from the way her body shuddered how difficult it was for her, but silently he prayed she would move faster. At any second they could be spotted!

Going as fast as the pain would allow her, and careful not to make any noise, Kelly slowly hauled herself up the ladder until finally she made it to the roof. Then she slid forward noiselessly out of sight.

Jess gestured at Billy Joe to climb up next. Billy Joe took one last look around to make sure none of the gunmen could see him, then he began to make his way up too. He took it slow, careful not to make any noise. He reached the top and then slid himself silently along the wooden roof and joined Kelly where she was hidden among the bales of cloth. She was half-sitting half-lying, propped up against one of the bales. Her face was deathly white.

She's gonna die, thought Billy Joe. *She's gonna try and save her kids and she's gonna die.*

Jess joined them soon after, sliding quietly along

the roof. Billy Joe found a gap between two of the bales and looked down at the scene by the tents.

Jimmy Flynn and Robert had tied up Scrub, and had released Jeb. They now stood holding Jeb at gunpoint.

'OK, your man's free!' called Jimmy Flynn.

Then Flynn and Robert retreated back to the cover of the bushes and the undergrowth.

There was the sound of a door below being unlocked and opened, and then Rixon's voice was heard saying, 'Who's there?'

'It's me, Jeb!' The gunman called back.

'OK!' shouted Rixon. 'Now you people listen out! Dan here and Jeb are gonna hitch up the horses to this wagon. I'll have my gun aimed at these two kids the whole time. If anyone starts shootin', the kids get it!'

'No one's gonna start shootin', so long as you don't!' Flynn called back.

There was a pause, then Rixon called out, 'Where's that woman gunfighter? Why ain't she doin' the talkin' no more?'

'Cos she don't trust you!' Jimmy Flynn called back. 'She's found herself a good position and she's sittin' there right now with a rifle aimed at that wagon. If you or your men try any sneaky stuff, she's gonna start shootin'. An' you know what a good shot she is!'

'We ain't gonna try nothin'!' Rixon shouted. 'All we

wanna do is get outta here.' There was a pause, then he called out, 'OK, Jeb, Dan's comin' out! You two get that team of horses fixed up and let's get goin'!'

Then there was the sound of boots on the steps. Billy Joe strained to look down, not daring to put his face too far out in case he was spotted. He saw Dan and Jeb lead the horses to the wagon and hitch them up. With two of them working together, it didn't take long.

'The team's ready, Duke!' called Dan.

'OK!' called Rixon. 'You and Jeb get up on the seat and get this thing movin'.'

'Rixon's making sure he stays inside,' whispered Jess. 'He ain't gonna show his face till we're well away. He still thinks you'd shoot him if he was up front holding the reins.'

'And he'd be right,' muttered Kelly darkly. 'If I had him in my gunsights that man would be dead for sure.'

'When you gonna let those kids go?' shouted Ed Bartlett.

'About two miles down the road!' Rixon called back. 'You can come and find 'em in a couple of hours. If we see any riders comin' after us, the kids die!'

'No one's gonna be comin' after you!' Jimmy Flynn assured him.

'OK, let's go!' called Rixon.

On the roof, Billy Joe heard the sound of the door of the wagon being shut. Jeb called out, 'Ho!' and the reins were flicked along the team of four horses. Then the wagon began to roll. They were on their way.

CHAPTER 21

The wagon rocked and jumped as it went along, shaking the boys on the roof. They clung to the ropes holding the bales of cloth and wooden crates in place, determined not to be rattled loose and thrown off.

Billy Joe shot a glance towards Kitty Kelly as she lay, her face pale and her eyes closed, a pistol in her hand.

'Think she's dead?' asked Billy Joe in a worried whisper.

Jess looked towards her, then shook his head.

'No,' he said. 'I'm sure I saw her breathe.'

Billy Joe was doubtful.

'I didn't see it,' he said. 'Anyway, if she ain't dead yet, she sure looks like she ain't far off it.'

'She'll be OK,' whispered Jess. 'Let's go see what's happenin' at the front.'

Billy Joe and Jess wriggled forward along the roof of the moving wagon. Billy Joe shot another glance at Kitty Kelly. She still hadn't moved. Luckily, one of her arms was caught between a bale and one of the tying ropes, holding her on the roof as the wagon jumped and bucked.

The two boys got to the front and peered down carefully. Below, Dan was at the reins, urging the team of four horses along as fast as they could go. Jeb sat beside him, a rifle cradled in his arms.

Jess slid back.

'I got an idea,' he said. He gestured at the bales and wooden crates lashed to the roof near them. 'We drop a coupla crates on 'em, they'll knock 'em out and push 'em off the wagon. Then I'll jump down and grab the reins and turn the wagon back towards the goldfields.'

Billy Joe peered over the edge of the roof at the two gunmen below, then turned back to Jess.

'Say we drop the crates and miss 'em?' he asked.

Jess shrugged. 'The crates are pretty large, and those guys ain't moving around much,' he said. 'It's a chance we gotta take. I ain't shootin' those men in the back of the head for no reason, Billy Joe. They ain't killed no one.'

Billy Joe nodded.

'I reckon you're right,' he agreed.

The two boys worked their way back to the nearest crates. Jess pulled out his knife and set to work, sawing through the ropes that fixed them to the roof. Once two were free, the boys slid them to the front of the wagon. They took one last careful look at Dan and Jeb below. Both gunmen were intent on watching the road ahead, and every now and then Jeb peered round the side of the stage to see if they were being followed. Neither man looked up.

Jess looked at Billy Joe and then nodded. The boys began to push the crates forward. Suddenly the wagon gave a lurch, and the crates slid forward and then toppled, nearly pulling the two boys over the edge. Just in time they managed to untangle their hands from the ropes, and the crates fell. Then there were two sickening thuds. The boys inched forward. Both men were gone. Billy Joe raised himself up and looked back. Dan and Jeb were lying spreadeagled on the ground in the distance, the two crates close by.

'What was that?!' shouted Rixon, his voice muffled from inside the wagon. 'What was that noise? We hit somethin' or what?'

'Nothin,' Jess grunted back, keeping his voice low and hoping he'd fool Rixon.

Jess slid forward, held onto the edge of the roof, then dropped down onto the wooden seat at the front of the wagon, scooping up the reins. The team of horses barely seemed to notice; they were heading along at a fast pace. Jess reined them in slightly, then pulled on the left-hand reins and began to turn the horses round.

'What's goin' on?! Why are we turning?' shouted Rixon again.

Jess glanced up at Billy Joe and the boys exchanged looks of helplessness. Maybe they could fool Rixon with one grunted word, but if they tried giving him a longer answer, he'd know it was them for sure.

'Answer me!' raged Rixon.

There was silence, then Billy Joe heard Rixon snap at Shane and Em, 'I'm goin' up top to see what's happenin'. You two kids stay here! If you try any funny business, I'll shoot you through the wood of the roof! It's tight enough in here that I'll surely hit one of yer.'

Billy Joe's heart gave a leap of fear. Rixon was coming up onto the roof! He slid over to where Kitty Kelly lay. She still hadn't moved and looked like she was dead, then he saw her mouth open slightly. She was still breathing, but she was no use to him right now. She was out cold.

Below, Billy Joe heard the rear door of the wagon open, and the sound of boots on the ladder. Rixon was coming up, and he'd sure as shootin' have a loaded gun ready in his hand!

CHAPTER 22

Billy Joe felt panic surge through him. Rixon's head had appeared and he was looking at Billy Joe in shock. Then the man acted. He pulled himself up, levelled his gun at Billy Joe and fired.

Bang!

Billy Joe had started to throw himself to one side as he saw Rixon level his gun, and the bullet missed and tore into one of the bales of cloth. Frantically Billy Joe slid to where Kitty Kelly lay and grabbed at the pistol held in her hand. For a second the pistol stuck. Kelly's fingers seemed clamped firmly around the butt. Desperately, Billy Joe tugged at the pistol, and finally it came loose, sending him sliding backwards across the roof with the effort. It was lucky for Billy Joe that it did because Rixon's next shot went through the wood of the roof, right where the boy had been lying.

Billy Joe swung the gun up and fired blindly, just as

Rixon was swinging his pistol to point at Billy Joe again. Billy Joe's bullet hit Rixon in the shoulder and he yelled out in pain and stumbled back, and then toppled and fell. The gunman fired one last shot, but the bullet missed Billy Joe and again smashed through the wood of the roof, then Rixon disappeared over the edge of the wagon.

'Shane!' yelled Billy Joe. 'You OK?'

'Th-that you, B-Billy Joe?' came Shane's voice.

'Sure is!' Billy Joe called back. 'And Jess is at the reins drivin' the horses! We're gonna be OK!'

'There's f-fire here!' yelled Shane. 'Those b-bullets h-hit s-somethin' and it's on f-fire!'

The gunpowder! thought Billy Joe. *It'll kill us all*!

Billy Joe slid to the front and shouted frantically down to Jess.

'Jess! There's fire inside the wagon! Cut the horses loose and jump clear!' Then he shouted, 'Shane! You take Em and jump out!'

Jess pulled on the reins, shouting, 'Ho!' at the horses and pulling on the brake to bring the wagon to a halt. Billy Joe saw him pull out his knife and jump down and start cutting at the leather of the reins.

Already Billy Joe could hear the crackling of flames. He wondered how near they were to the gunpowder. If the fire was next to it, he had no time at all. He'd be dead within seconds, as soon as it blew.

He slid across to where Kitty Kelly lay, still

unconscious. He had to try to save her. After years apart, Shane and his ma had found one another, and Billy Joe was going to make sure they didn't lose each other again.

He threw the pistol to the ground, then grabbed Kelly beneath the arms and started to pull her along the roof towards the ladder.

If she ain't dead already, this could kill her, he thought. He reached the rear of the roof and looked down. Shane and Em had scrambled out and were standing a short distance from the wagon.

'J-jump, Billy Joe!' called Shane. 'It's g-gonna b-blow up!'

'I got your ma here!' called back Billy Joe.

'M-Ma!' shouted Shane, and he ran towards the wagon.

'Get back!' yelled Billy Joe. 'Look after Em!'

But Shane ignored him and ran to the ladder.

'L-lower her d-down!' he called. 'I'll t-take her!'

Billy Joe hauled the unconscious body of Kelly so that it was balanced on the edge of the roof, and then he began to lower her down, holding onto her arms as tightly as he could. She was a dead weight and he felt the sockets of his arms being strained, as if they might pop out at any moment.

'I can't hold on!' he yelled.

'D-drop her!' said Shane. 'Quick!'

Billy Joe lowered Kelly a bit further, as much as he

could without falling himself, and then he released his grip. He saw Shane step beneath her and fall under her weight, and then struggle to his feet and begin to drag her away from the wagon.

Billy Joe could see the smoke now, belching out black, and feel the heat of the flames that had caught on the wooden sides of the store. The whole wagon was raging with fire! He swung off the edge of the roof and dropped down the last few rungs of the ladder to the ground. He fell, then stumbled to his feet and ran to join Shane. He took one of Kelly's arms while Shane used both hands to hold onto her other arm, and they dragged her along the dusty and uneven ground as fast as they could. Billy Joe looked round to find Em.

'Run!' he shouted at her.

The little girl turned and ran.

Billy Joe shot a look back towards the wagon. The flames were now climbing higher up the sides, turning it into a raging inferno. Thick smoke billowed away from it. Suddenly Billy Joe heard the sound of hooves approaching fast. He turned and saw that Jess was riding on one of the horses, coming towards them.

'Get Em away!' Billy Joe yelled at Jess. He pointed at the small girl.

He wasn't sure if Jess had heard above the roar and crackle of the flames, and the thud of the horse's hooves, but Jess had obviously had the same thought. He pulled the horse up alongside Em and reached down for her, then swung the little girl up behind him.

Jess was just about to ride away when a shot rang out and the horse squealed and reared up in fright, throwing Jess and Em to the ground.

Billy Joe whirled round and saw Rixon stumbling towards them. He was covered in dust and bleeding from when he'd fallen from the roof of the wagon.

'You ain't gonna live! None of you!' he roared.

Suddenly there was a deafening *WHOOMPFFF*! as the gunpowder inside the wagon exploded. Billy Joe threw himself to the ground instinctively as shards of wood and metal flew towards him. They passed over him, leaving an echo of heat in the air, then he was covered in dust as the cloud of smoke enveloped him.

Billy Joe lay still for a few moments, his ears ringing from the deafening sound of the explosion. He felt himself, checking for injuries or burnt clothing, but he seemed to have survived.

He was glad of the dust cloud. It would blind Rixon, prevent him getting a fix on them and taking a shot. He pushed himself to his feet and stumbled towards where he'd last seen Shane. He bumped into his friend bending over the still form of Kitty Kelly.

'I th-think she's d-dead!' Shane sobbed.

Billy Joe bent down and put his ear to Kelly's mouth.

'No, she ain't,' he said. 'She's very weak, but she's still alive. And we gotta get her safe before Rixon finds us!'

Billy Joe saw Kelly's pistol lying on the ground and snatched it up. Now the dust cloud was settling, the air around them was clearing and he could make out dim shapes. Jess stood holding onto the reins of the horses, calming them down. Behind him, holding onto his coat, was Em.

Where was Rixon? If Billy Joe could see Jess, then Rixon could surely see all of them.

As the dust settled onto the ground and the smoke finally cleared, Billy Joe saw Rixon at last. He was lying on his back on the ground with something sticking out of him. He wasn't moving.

Billy Joe crept forward, making his way carefully, the pistol in his hand firmly pointing at the still form of Rixon on the ground.

But Rixon didn't move. As Billy Joe got nearer he could see why. Rixon was dead. A miner's pickaxe had been blown out of the store wagon with the explosion and the metal spike had hit Rixon in the chest. The pickaxe stuck up into the air from Rixon's body.

Billy Joe lowered the gun, and was aware of Jess joining him, little Em by his side.

'Rixon?' asked Jess.

'Dead,' said Billy Joe. Suddenly he felt weak from it all. He shook his head to stop himself from collapsing right there. 'We did it, Jess,' he said. 'We saved Shane and Em, and we beat the bad guys.'

Jess looked towards where Shane was kneeling

beside the still body of Kitty Kelly.

'What about Shane's ma?' he asked.

Billy Joe hesitated.

'I don't know,' he admitted. 'I told Shane she was still alive, but I ain't so sure. I think gettin' her off the wagon the way we did may have moved that bullet.' He shook his head sadly. 'I don't think we managed to save her after all.'

CHAPTER 23

Billy Joe, Jess, Shane and Andy stood in the cemetery as the preacher said the words over the grave. Little Em stood beside Shane, holding his hand. Patch stood beside Andy. It had been a short service, with the preacher saying a few words about the deceased. There were very few other people at the graveside, but then Billy Joe hadn't really expected there to be.

'Ashes to ashes, dust to dust,' said the preacher. 'May the soul of the departed rest in peace.'

Then he nodded to the gravediggers who were standing nearby, and they began shovelling earth into the grave on the coffin.

'Let's go,' muttered Jess.

As the four boys, the little girl and the dog made their way out of the cemetery and walked along the track that would take them back to their town of Drygulch, Andy complained, 'I can't see why we had to come. He tried to kill us!'

'I just wanted to make sure he was really dead,' grunted Billy Joe. 'I wouldn't trust Duke Rixon not to spring up out of that grave and start shootin' at us again.'

'What about the other two?' asked Andy.

'Jeb and Dan,' nodded Jess. 'There was no sign of them when the posse went lookin'.'

'Just the two crates lyin' there,' added Billy Joe.

'So they're still out there somewhere,' said Andy. 'You think they'll come and find us an' kill us after what we done to Rixon?'

'We didn't do nothin',' said Billy Joe sharply. 'He got killed by a pickaxe.'

'And no one's gonna come after us,' added Jess. 'We got protection. Ain't that right, Shane?'

Shane grinned broadly.

'S-sure is!' he said. And he looked down fondly at his little sister, who was hurrying along by his side, determined to keep up with her big brother and his friends.

They arrived at the small town and headed towards one of the neat wooden houses at the edge of town. It had a low picket fence running round it, flowers growing in the front garden, and a sign by the front gate saying 'Johnson'.

The boys and Em and the dog walked up the path to the front door. It opened as they got near and Amos

Johnson, a friend and neighbour of the boys, looked out at them with a smile.

'Your ma's in the bedroom with Mrs Johnson,' he said to Shane.

'Th-. thank you, Mr J-Johnson,' stammered Shane, and he guided Em into the house and towards the bedroom at the back.

'You boys wanna come inside?' asked Mr Johnson.

'Thank you, Mr Johnson, but we'll be happy sitting out here on the porch and waiting for Shane, if that's OK by you,' said Jess.

'That's fine by me,' nodded Johnson. 'In fact, I think I'll join you.'

Jess and Billy Joe settled themselves down on a bench, along with Mr Johnson, while Andy went running off to play with Patch.

'How was the service?' asked Johnson.

'Considerin' Duke Rixon was a cold-hearted varmint with no conscience about killin' women and children, I think the preacher done good by him,' said Billy Joe, loosening his collar.

Inside the house, Shane and Em entered the back bedroom. Their mother lay in the bed, Mrs Johnson standing beside it mopping her brow with water. Kitty Kelly looked pale, but she smiled when she saw her son and daughter.

'I'll leave you together,' said Mrs Johnson, adding, 'But remember what Doc Benson said – no getting excited. So you just lay there and talk for a little while, then you got to get some more rest.'

With that, Mrs Johnson left the room, stopping at the door to say to Shane firmly, 'Remember what I just said. Your ma's got to rest. So you spend just a few minutes with her. That clear?'

Shane nodded.

'That's c-clear, th-thank you, Mrs J-Johnson,' he said.

He sat down on the chair beside the bed, and moved along so that Em could join him.

'You both OK?' asked Kelly, her voice faint.

'We sure are,' nodded Em. 'Shane and the boys are takin' real good care of me. Theirs is a real nice house, Ma. You ought to come and see it soon as you're up.'

Kelly looked at her son and smiled.

'I don't know what we'd have done without your friends,' she said. 'If it hadn't been for Jess and Billy Joe, we'd all have been dead for sure.'

Shane nodded and smiled back.

'Th-that's what they do,' he said. 'S-save people.' He looked at his ma, and then said, 'The d-doc says you're g-gonna be OK, once you get your strength b-back.'

'That's right,' she said.

'Wh-what will you d-do?' he asked. 'W-will you st-stay here?'

There was a thoughtful silence, then Kelly said, 'I don't know, Shane. I got a job to do.'

'And it n-nearly got you k-killed,' said Shane.

'I know,' she answered. 'But if I hadn't come to those goldfields to do my job, I'd never have found you again.'

'But n-now you've f-found me, you ain't g-got to look for me n-no more,' said Shane.

Kelly smiled.

'That's true,' she said. She closed her eyes momentarily, then opened them again and looked at him. 'I don't want to lose you again, Shane. If I do move on, you can come with me.'

Shane fell silent, then he smiled.

'Yeah,' he said. He saw how pale she was, beads of sweat appearing on her forehead again. 'You're g-getting t-tired, Ma. You n-need to sl-sleep.' He stood up and took Em's hand. 'Come on, Em. W-we'll see M-Ma l-later.'

She nodded faintly, and then closed her eyes and sank back into her pillows.

When Shane got outside he let go of Em's hand, and immediately she ran to join Andy and Patch who were rolling over and over wrestling in the dust.

'She's a real tomboy,' observed Mr Johnson.

'Sh-she sure is,' agreed Shane.

'Your ma awake, Shane?' asked Billy Joe.

'Sh-she was. Sh-she's sleeping n-now.'

'You thought about what you're gonna do?' asked Billy Joe. 'If she moves on, that is.'

'That's too soon to be talkin' about that, Billy Joe,'

Jess rebuked him sharply. 'Let her get better first.'

'OK,' shrugged Billy Joe. 'I was just askin'.' He fell silent for a moment, then said, 'We goin' back to the goldfields?'

Jess looked at Andy, Em and Patch, tugging at one another and laughing out loud, and at Shane and Billy Joe on the bench seat next to him on the porch, and thought of Kitty Kelly recovering in the clean and comfortable bed in the house behind them. The dirt and hard work of the goldfields seemed a long way away. And although there were rumoured to have been small signs of gold for some folk, for the gang there had been nothing but blisters and sweat and near getting themselves killed. Gold-mining, Jess concluded, was more trouble than it was worth.

He shook his head.

'Nope,' he said. 'Guess we'll stay here in Drygulch.'

And then he saw light glint on something small that Andy was playing with, tossing it up in the air in the palm of his hand, and Jess felt his throat go dry. He swallowed hard.

'Andy!' he called. 'What's that you got?'

'Just a bit of rock I picked up when we was prospectin',' said Andy.

'Bring it over here!' called Jess.

Andy got up from the ground and ambled over to Jess, Shane and Billy Joe, Em and Patch following him. Billy Joe looked at the small piece of rock the young boy held out to Jess.

'I thought it might be gold, but it's just a lump of dirt with a shiny bit in it,' said Andy.

'Gold *is* dirt, Andy,' said Jess, taking the piece of rock and examining it. 'It don't only come in big lumps. It comes in tiny bits stuck to other rock.'

Billy Joe looked at the lump of dirt, awed.

'You ain't thinkin' –' he breathed.

Jess's face widened into a huge smile.

'Boys,' he announced. 'I think Andy done struck gold!'

Look out for more BADLANDS books
by Eldridge James . . .

Boys grow up fast in the west

BADLANDS
DEATH IN DRYGULCH

ELDRIDGE JAMES

BADLANDS
DEATH IN DRYGULCH

*Discover why Billy Joe came to Drygulch and
how he became one of the gang. . .*

There were shouts and screams from both
inside and outside the saloon, but Billy Joe was
already running as fast as he could. Then there
was another gunshot and he felt this bullet tear at
his jacket. The next one would blow him apart.

Billy Joe saw his father being gunned down.
Now the killers are after him.

The Drygulch gang have promised to save him
but they are only boys. Can they really protect
him from a ruthless band of desperadoes? His life
depends on it!

FIRST IN THE EXCITING BADLANDS SERIES BY
ELDRIDGE JAMES

The open range is a dangerous place

BADLANDS RANGE WARS

ELDRIDGE JAMES

BADLANDS
RANGE WARS

'Get your hands in the air! Keep your guns
on 'em, men! If they move, shoot 'em!'
The boys stared in shock at the man in the
light brown suit and the two cowboys
holding pistols pointed at them.
'What's goin' on?' demanded Jess angrily.
'We ain't done nothin'!'

*When the Drygulch gang are thrown out of the shack
they call home, they have to move on – but they soon
find themselves caught up in a deadly range war . . .*

SECOND IN THE EXCITING BADLANDS SERIES BY
ELDRIDGE JAMES

For more information about Badlands
or to find out more about other great
Catnip titles go to:

www.catnippublishing.co.uk